SUMMER WARPATH

Center Point
Large Print

Also by Wayne D. Overholser and available from Center Point Large Print:

Black Mike
The Durango Stage
Proud Journey
The Trouble Kid
Pass Creek Valley

**This Large Print Book carries the
Seal of Approval of N.A.V.H.**

SUMMER WARPATH

Wayne D. Overholser

CENTER POINT LARGE PRINT
THORNDIKE, MAINE

This Circle Ⓥ Western is published by
Center Point Large Print in the year 2017 in
co-operation with Golden West Literary Agency.

First Edition
January, 2017

Printed in the United States of America
on permanent paper.
Set in 16-point Times New Roman type.

ISBN: 978-1-68324-250-5

Library of Congress Cataloging-in-Publication Data

Names: Overholser, Wayne D., 1906–1996, author.
Title: Summer warpath : a Circle V Western / Wayne D. Overholser.
Description: First edition. | Thorndike, Maine : Center Point Large
    Print, 2017.
Identifiers: LCCN 2016042176 | ISBN 9781683242505
    (hardcover : alk. paper)
Subjects: LCSH: Large type books. | GSAFD: Western stories.
Classification: LCC PS3529.V33 S855 2017 | DDC 813/.54—dc23
LC record available at https://lccn.loc.gov/2016042176

CHAPTER ONE

The day was April 20, 1876, the kind of warm spring day that makes a man feel life is being born again on the prairie. Here and there a hint of green appeared in the grass and the buds of the cotton-woods along the creek were starting to swell. But it was a day, too, when death might be waiting in any ravine.

Funny how a man senses danger, Walt Staley thought. *Sometimes it's an uneasy prickle between the shoulder blades. Sometimes it's a faint chill sliding along the spine. Today it's a coldness deep in my belly.*

He stopped in the bottom of a shallow valley and let his buckskin drink.

Both the Sioux and the Cheyennes were ugly this spring. The way Staley saw it, they had a right to be, but his sympathy wouldn't save his hair if a war party crossed his trail. He had ridden most of the night and on into the morning. Now he was dead tired. So was his buckskin, but he couldn't stop, even though he had finished the last of his grub yesterday morning.

The question that had been nagging him for several hours was whether he should hide until dark, or try to make it to Fort Laramie, twenty-five or thirty miles away. A third choice was Louie

Barrone's horse ranch. He decided to head for Louie's.

Early that morning he had passed the site of an Indian camp. He'd guessed there had been eight or nine braves in the outfit. They had stayed one night and then ridden south, probably yesterday morning. He also guessed it was a war party because he had found part of the carcass of an antelope. If squaws had been along, they would have worked up all the meat; that, of course, was labor a brave could not be bothered with.

The prairie stretched out for miles on all sides of Staley. It made a long swell in front of him to the top of a ridge, and it sloped down on the other side to a brush-choked draw about like this one. If he got caught out here in the open by a band of Sioux or Cheyennes, he was a dead duck.

He rode across the shallow stream and started up the slope. Barrone's ranch was out of his way if he wanted to go on to Fort Laramie after dark, but there was no hurry. It had been a long time since Walt Staley had been in a hurry to go anywhere.

So he angled east, not pushing the buckskin at all. He'd get to Barrone's place easily by noon. He studied the brow of the hill ahead of him, then turned in his saddle and glanced behind him. Nothing moved, not even a bird or a jack rabbit. An empty land. The coldness still chilled his belly. Indians were near. They could be watching him right now.

An hour later he topped the ridge and looked down on Barrone's ranch, a low log building with a dirt roof, a log barn, and a pole corral. Barrone had lived here for twenty years. During that time the Indians had never been a serious problem to him, probably because he had married a Cheyenne squaw named White Bird when he'd settled down. White Bird had died two years ago, but Barrone still lived here with his boys, Bill and Joe, and his daughter Tally.

Staley put his horse down the slope. Might be smart to stay the night, he thought. Barrone would know if the Indians were moving in great enough numbers to be feared. Usually they gave him information they wouldn't give anyone else. Staley might be able to pick up news that General Crook would like to hear.

Reining up in front of the barn, he saw smoke rising from both the kitchen and the fireplace chimneys, but no other sign of human life. A mangy black dog that had been sleeping in the shade of the barn got up and moved away in a half circle, his ears down, his teeth showing as he expressed in a surly growl his displeasure over Staley's presence. Half a dozen nondescript hens were scratching industriously in the manure pile on the other side of the corral. They ignored his arrival and continued to scratch.

Staley dismounted, wondering if Barrone and the boys had left for the day. He hoped so. He hadn't seen Tally since fall, and even then he hadn't had much of a chance to talk to her. Barrone guarded her closely and his sons would skin any man alive who laid a hand on her.

Several times during the previous summer and fall Staley had stopped here for a meal and had camped in the willows below the house. Tally liked him well enough to slip out during the night and visit him.

In front of her father and brothers she was a demure and innocent girl who kept her real feelings hidden behind an Indian-like mask. She hated her life and she had let Staley know that she would go away with him any time he would take her. He was tempted, but he didn't like the prospect of having Louie Barrone and the boys on his trail for the rest of his life.

Staley was still standing beside his buckskin, his gaze on the house, when the boys appeared in the barn doorway. They moved toward him in their graceful, cat-like way. Bill was nineteen, Joe eighteen, and they were exactly the same size and looked enough alike to be twins. They had the high cheek bones, dark eyes, and black hair of their mother, and the light skin of their father.

Neither spoke. They came directly at him, scowling, right hands resting on the butts of their guns.

When they reached him, Bill said: "Pap's in the

house. He'll ask you to dinner when he sees you, so put your horse away."

"Don't say nothing to Tally," Joe said.

"If you do, I'll cut your god-damned heart out," Bill said.

"And I'll eat it," Joe said.

They went on to the house, neither looking back. Staley watched them until they disappeared into the kitchen. Half-breeds lived in a world of their own. Because they were not accepted by either whites or Indians, they were fiercely loyal to each other. Staley had seen this loyalty demonstrated many times, and had supposed that the Barrone boys' protective attitude toward Tally stemmed from it. Now he sensed something else, but he wasn't sure what it was.

He stripped gear from his buckskin and turned him into the corral, then started toward the house. Louie Barrone came striding out of the kitchen, bellowing: "Where the hot and living hell did you drop from, Walt?"

He was a giant of a man, this Louie Barrone. He went back to the days of Ashley and Broken Hand Fitzpatrick and Jedediah Smith and Bill Sublette and Jim Bridger and the rest of the mountain men who had made history in the 1820s and 1830s.

As far as Staley knew, the old man was the only one who survived. He had a magnificent white beard and mustache, and his hair, equally white, fell to his shoulders. Some men, such as Buffalo

Bill Cody, who wore their hair long struck Staley as being frauds, but not Louie Barrone.

Staley shook hands, grinning a little. "You look like you wintered in pretty good shape, Louie."

"I did, I did," Barrone said. "We ain't seen hide nor hair of you for six, seven months. Where'd you winter?"

"On the Yellowstone with the Crows," Staley said.

"The Crows!" Barrone snorted his disgust. "A bunch o' chicken-livered, stealin' female Injuns. That's what they are. Couldn't you do no better'n that?"

"They ain't that bad, Louie," Staley said. "I get along pretty well with 'em. Besides, I didn't know any Cheyennes or Sioux who'd welcome me."

"Well, now that is the truth. They've turned mean and that's a fact." Barrone threw a hand out in a sweeping gesture toward the prairie. "They're thicker'n fleas all over this country. Half a dozen bands have ridden past here in the last week. Always before they'd stop and palaver, but this spring they're all painted up for war and they ride right on by."

"It saves feeding 'em," Staley said.

"I'd rather feed 'em than have 'em steal from me. We usually have a buffalo hump or a hunk of antelope to give 'em. Fact is, White Bird always liked to jaw with 'em when they stopped. The boys still do." The old man shook his head, his beard flying in the breeze. "I dunno, Walt. These are bad days. In the twenty years I've lived here, I don't figger I've lost ten head of horses to the Injuns. White outlaws have robbed me plenty of times, but not Injuns."

It wasn't Louis Barrone's way to worry, Staley thought. He was not a man to work hard. He'd never had to. He'd lived off the country, and if and when he needed money, he'd round up some of his horses and drive them to Fort Fetterman or Fort Laramie and once in a while as far south as Fort D.A. Russell. But now something more than robbery by the Indians was bothering him.

"You may have bad trouble, all right," Staley said. "The Sioux and Cheyennes are going to need horses if they fight as big a war as I think they're going to."

"Sure they will," Barrone said. "This Black Hills business has made 'em ornery. Like kicking a beehive. It's damned funny how the government makes a treaty with the Injuns who are s'posed to keep it, but the white men can break it any time they want to." He waggled a finger at Staley. "The government wants a war. You can be dead sure of that. Only way to get the Black Hills. Uncle Sam's got to whip the Sioux and make 'em sign another treaty. That's the ticket."

Staley nodded. The discovery of gold in the Black Hills was going to get a lot of folks killed.

Barrone slapped him on the back. "Well, come on in. I told Tally to heave another antelope steak into the pot. It's probably done afore this, and here we are, standing out here jawing."

Staley followed the old man into the kitchen.

CHAPTER TWO

Tally was frying meat at the stove. She did not speak or look around or indicate in any way that she knew Staley was there. He glanced at her brothers. They were sitting at the table, leaning forward, tense, their hands hidden below table level.

Suddenly it struck Staley that the boys were holding their revolvers on their laps. If he even spoke to Tally, it would be enough to provoke the boys into shooting him. All they needed was an excuse.

Something was wrong in the Barrone family, something desperately wrong that was barely hidden beneath the surface. Staley hung his hat on a peg near the door. Whatever happened, he would lean over backward to avoid a fight.

"Come on and sit," Louie Barrone boomed. "I reckon you're hungry."

"Yeah, my tapeworm has been howling for quite a spell," Staley admitted as he sat down on a bench across from the boys.

Tally brought a platter of meat to the table. She returned to the stove and came back with the coffee pot and filled the tin cups. She fetched potatoes, biscuits, and a pitcher of molasses.

The boys started to eat, picking up slices of meat

and tearing off great hunks with their teeth. Blood and grease ran down their chins, but it didn't bother them or slow them up. Joe stopped long enough to produce a great, rumbling belch, then went on eating.

Staley was not a fussy man. You didn't spend a winter with the Crows if you were. Still, the boys' table manners bothered him. He had never seen them eat this way before.

He watched them, and his memory stirred. Once he had watched a couple of hungry Indian boys after they downed a buffalo. They had cut the buffalo open, pulled out its liver, dripping warm blood and still quivering with life, and eaten it raw. So that was it. Joe and Bill Barrone were trying to act like Indians.

Staley ate slowly, hoping the boys would finish and leave the table. He glanced casually at Tally. She had filled out since fall. She had the features of a white woman. The blue-black hair and light copper skin made a fine setting for those slanting blue eyes.

Tally was tall, almost as tall as her brothers, and she would never look dumpy as so many squaws did in middle life. She was clean, her hair was brushed and pinned at the back of her head, and, in spite of the loose-fitting calico dress, she seemed very much a woman.

The boys finished eating, but they remained at the table, their faces inscrutable, their eyes fixed on Staley. He pretended that he didn't notice. He had to figure out a way to see Tally before he went on to Fort Laramie.

It occurred to him suddenly that Tally would be the kind of wife he wanted. He had not thought about it before because he had always considered her a girl. But now she was more than that.

Most folks would call him a fool for even thinking of taking a wife. He had no job and no money. He owned nothing except his buckskin, his saddle, his Winchester, and a sack of shells. He was a pilgrim who never stayed with a job for more than a month at a time, and the woman he married would have to be a wanderer, too. But Tally wouldn't mind. He was sure of it.

"Coffee." Barrone nodded at Tally and wiped a sleeve across his mouth. "What are you fixing to do, Walt? If you're looking for a job, I'll give you one."

"No," Joe said sharply. "We can do all the riding that's got to be done."

Barrone glared at his son. "The old dog is still running this outfit," he bellowed. "Not the pups." He turned to Staley. "How about it, Walt?"

"I ain't looking for that kind of a job," Staley said carefully. "I'll know what I want to do when I get to the fort. Several things ought to be opening up this time of year."

Tally brought the coffee pot, filled the cups

again, and took the pot back to the stove. She moved gracefully without making a sound.

"Yeah, I reckon you ought to find something you want," Barrone said. "I never figgered you being too particular."

"No, not as long as the pay's good and there's enough of a risk to make it interesting," Staley said.

Barrone slurped his coffee and put his cup down. "Since you was here last fall, a hog ranch has started up between here and the fort. A woman calling herself Madame Fifi brought some girls up from Cheyenne. She's bigger'n a buffalo cow, but her girls ain't so bad. She's got one purty little heifer she calls Christine. Claims the girl's her niece. Maybe she is. All I know is, none of the men get into bed with her."

"And they all try," Staley said.

Barrone guffawed. "Sure they do, but you can bet they ain't getting past Madame Fifi."

Tally had returned to her chair. She sat down, her gaze on her empty plate. She had gone to school in Cheyenne, coming back to stay only after her mother died, so she knew how civilized people lived and how they talked in front of their women. Now she was embarrassed because she knew that Staley knew.

"Anything else between here and the fort?" Staley asked to change the subject.

"Yeah, there's an Army hay camp on the north

16

prong of Squaw Creek," Barrone said. "They must have put up three hundred tons of hay last summer. They haul it to the fort when they need it. I guess they got six, eight men there."

The old man rose. "Saddle up, boys. Time we was moving out." He turned to Staley who was on his feet. "I don't ride as well as I used to, but I want to see if I got any horses left."

"You're a good cook, Tally," Staley said. "Thanks for the dinner."

"You're welcome," Tally said, her gaze still on her plate.

Both boys remained on the bench, acting as if they hadn't heard their father's order. Barrone started toward the back door. Then, realizing the boys hadn't moved, he wheeled back to face them.

"Didn't you hear me?" he roared. "I said saddle up. We're riding."

Both boys stared at him defiantly. Bill said: "No. We ain't riding as long as this bastard's in the house with Tally."

Barrone hit Bill on the mouth with an open palm. The sound of the slap seemed to fill the room, and it knocked Bill to the floor. Barrone moved fast for a man of his age. He would have hit Joe if the younger boy hadn't slid off the end of the bench. Joe backed away, right hand on the butt of his gun.

Barrone said: "Get your hand off that iron before I take it away from you and ram it down

17

your throat. Then get out to the corral and saddle up like I told you."

Bill came to his feet, blood trickling down his chin from the corner of his mouth. For a moment the boys stood motionless, facing their father, their dark eyes hot with rage. Then without a word they strode toward the back door.

Barrone watched them until the door closed, then took a deep breath. "It's been a long time since I whupped 'em, but I'm going to have to do it again."

"I'll be riding," Staley said. "No use making 'em any madder at me than they are."

"They got no call to get mad at you," Barrone said. "I dunno what's got into 'em."

For just a moment Staley's gaze touched Tally's face while Barrone was still glaring at the back door. She glanced up and whispered: "Wait for me." He nodded and left the room. Barrone followed him.

Outside, Barrone said: "I tell you, Walt, these are bad days when your own boys want to turn Injun. I told 'em I'd kill 'em if they done it, but I don't figger that's gonna stop 'em."

They walked toward the corral. Staley understood how the old man felt, but the day was past when Louie Barrone could handle his sons as he chose. The old man should realize it, and Staley wanted to tell him, but he knew he could not.

"I sure rue the day I brought White Bird here,"

Barrone said gloomily. "A 'breed ain't got no chance in this country. The whites won't take 'em and neither will the Injuns unless they live the Injun way. And there's no future in being an Injun. The Army's gonna chase 'em this summer till their tails are dragging." He wiped a hand across his mouth, then he said: "The thing is, I don't want my kids living like Injuns and I ain't gonna stand still for it."

For an instant Staley was tempted to tell Barrone that he wanted to marry Tally. But this was not the time. He had to talk to Tally first.

He went on to the corral and saddled the buckskin, ignoring the boys. He mounted and said: "I'll be by again sometime, Louie. So long."

"So long," Barrone said.

Staley rode south. When he looked back a few minutes later, he saw Barrone and his sons riding west. Staley did not look at them again until he reached the crest of the ridge. By that time the Barrone riders were three dots far up the valley.

Staley topped the ridge and rode far enough down the south slope to be hidden from Barrone and his boys. He dismounted, loosened the cinch, let the reins drag, then sprawled on the grass to wait for Tally.

CHAPTER THREE

Tally came racing over the crest of the ridge. She rode a bay mare bareback, her calico dress pulled far up on her brown legs. She paused a moment, saw Staley, and came down the slope in a headlong run. She skidded to a stop and slid to the ground.

Staley got to his feet and grinned at her. He began: "Well, you sure . . ." And she threw herself at him. Her arms went tight around him, and she buried her face against his chest.

"I'm sorry I couldn't talk to you," she said in a muffled voice. "I wanted to, but I didn't dare. They'd have killed you."

"I got that notion," he said.

She threw her head back and looked at him. "Take me away, Walt. I'll go anywhere with you. I'll do anything. I don't care. Just take me away."

Staley stood motionless. They had never done anything more than hold hands last summer and fall. He'd kissed her when he left, but it hadn't been much of a kiss. Now she was gripping the front of his buckskin shirt, begging him to take her away. She hadn't said a word about getting married. Maybe it didn't make any difference.

"Now wait a minute," he said. "There's something we better talk about. I ain't one to settle down. I ain't one to work hard and save money, neither. I like to work a little here and a little there and drift around, maybe just sleep under the trees and fish and hunt and not work at all until I have to. I guess most folks would say I was just plain shiftless."

"I don't care," Tally cried. "I told you I'd go anywhere and do anything. I can't stay here any longer."

"Why?"

She released her grip on his shirt, turned, and walked away. She wiped her eyes and for a moment she just stood, staring down the draw. Then she faced him. "I didn't intend to throw myself at you, Walt. No man likes that, I guess, but you're the only decent man I know. Every day since the weather warmed up a little I've been watching for you, and then when you did come, I couldn't say a word to you."

"I still don't savvy why you can't stay here," Staley said. "You've kept house for your pa for two years. I don't see . . ."

"Oh Walt, you know what's happening. This is the summer of an Indian war. The Cheyennes are going right along with the Sioux, though they don't have as good a reason to fight. I'm half Indian. I'm not ashamed of it, but I can't and won't live like an Indian. I lived with a white family when I went to school and I worked for my room and board. Pa paid a little, but most of it I earned. I know there's something better than living like a squaw."

"You ain't living like a squaw," Staley said. "I still don't see . . ."

"You saw how my brothers are. They're crazy, but they didn't get that way by accident. They're sick of living between two worlds. They say they'd rather be Indians and die like men than get kicked around the way 'breeds are, so they're going to join a Cheyenne band. There's a man named Big Elk they've been talking to. He's been by here a dozen times in the last month."

"Your pa said the Indians don't stop and palaver like they used to when your mother was alive."

"That's right. But they do ride by, and Bill and Joe sneak out and talk to them. Pa doesn't know that." She came close again and laid her hands on Staley's arms. "Walt, they've promised Big Elk he can have me. I told them I'd kill myself before I'd live with an Indian, but they just laugh at me. They say a squaw doesn't have any choice. To them I'm a squaw. That's why you've got to take me away."

He stared thoughtfully at her. The boys might turn Indian. Half-breeds often found their true home among their red relatives. The Indian way of life with its freedom and adventure appealed to many young half-breeds. But for Joe and Bill to trade their sister off to an Indian as if she were a filly that belonged to them was another matter.

"Tally," he said finally, "I don't think they'll do it. They're just talking, that's all. Your pa wouldn't stand for it."

"Pa!" She said the word with biting contempt. "He can't stop them. He thinks he can still beat them like he's always done, but he can't any more. They're men, and aren't going to forget things he's done like hitting Bill today. They hate him, Walt."

"I got the idea they did," he said.

"They're going to kill him," she said. "I don't know when or how. I don't think they know themselves. But when the time comes, they will." Her eyes filled with tears. "Don't you see, Walt? You've got to take me away."

"Did you tell Louie what you've told me? About them killing him?"

"I told him, Walt, but he doesn't listen. I mean, he listens, but he doesn't hear. He doesn't think they'll do anything. He says what you just said, that they're only talking. He says when they get older and figure out that the ranch is going to be theirs someday, they'll act different."

Her fingers dug into his arms. "They won't, Walt. He doesn't even know his own boys." Suddenly she seemed to wilt as if she had given up. "I shouldn't be asking you to take me away. I don't have any hold on you. It's just that I thought you liked me a little."

"I do," he said quickly. "Today, while we were

eating dinner, I thought that you were just the kind of woman I need for a wife."

She smiled for the first time this day.

"I am a woman," she said. "I'm seventeen, you know. I'd like to be your wife even if my skin isn't white."

"Tally, that doesn't make any difference."

She shook her head. "Don't lie to me, Walt. It makes a lot of difference. Our children will be quarter Indian, and that's enough to show. You'd be ashamed of them just like Pa's ashamed of us. I'm his housekeeper. The boys ride for him. That's all we are to him. He doesn't pay us a nickel."

"I don't think he . . ." Staley stopped. He didn't really know how Louie Barrone felt toward his children. Maybe Tally did. "Look. You go back to your place. All we can do is to hope nothing will happen for a while."

"You mean you . . . you won't take me?"

"Not today. I haven't got a job, or money, or a place to take you. But just as soon as I can, I'll come for you and we'll get married, all fit and proper. I wouldn't want it any other way, Tally."

"I see," she said listlessly, and turned away. "Good bye, Walt."

He caught her by a shoulder and turned her back to face him. "You've got to believe me, Tally. I'll come for you. I'd take you now if I had any place to leave you. But I don't. I don't even have any relatives."

"I understand," she said.

But he knew she didn't. He pulled her to him and kissed her roughly.

"One more time, Tally . . . I *will* come for you."

"I'll be here," she said. "I don't have any other place to go."

She ran to her mare, mounted, and rode away, head down. She was crying. He watched her until she dropped over the ridge. Then he turned to his buckskin and swung into the saddle.

It was a hell of a courtship, he told himself as he rode slowly down the slope. He knew less about white women than he did red ones, and Tally knew nothing about either white or red men. All she had was a woman's intuition and the terrible fear that she would be turned over to an Indian brave.

He had almost reached the bottom of the valley when he noticed the tracks of a number of horses, unshod ones, headed south. He followed the tracks for a time. He found no flowing water in the creekbed in the bottom of the draw, but the dirt was soft.

Stepping down, he kneeled beside the tracks and studied them. There were eight braves in the party and he judged they had made these tracks before noon. If he hadn't stopped at Barrone's ranch for dinner, he might be dead by now.

He mounted and rode south, his gaze sweeping the ridge line south of him. He judged he was about fifteen miles from Fort Laramie. The chances looked better than good that the war party was between him and the fort, and he couldn't go back to Barrone's. What the hell should he do?

Then he remembered the Army hay camp on the north prong of Squaw Creek. It would be only three or four miles from here. He rode toward Squaw Creek.

Chapter Four

Staley reached the hay camp late in the afternoon, his shadow falling far behind him. Brown haystacks dotted the valley. He was riding directly into the sun, and even with his hat brim pulled low over his eyes, he could not see clearly very far ahead of him.

Suddenly two of the brown mounds on his right became log buildings, not haystacks. He reined toward them, and saw that one was the house where the soldiers lived, the other a stable. Several soldiers were lounging in front of the house, all standing up and watching him approach except one, who sat near the far end, leaning against the wall, whittling.

Staley dismounted and let the reins drag. He said—"Howdy."—and waited.

The soldier at the end of the building kept on whittling. The rest just stood and stared. Staley's face turned red, but then another soldier appeared in the doorway, a young fellow about twenty-two or -three, well built and good-looking.

"Howdy," the young soldier said. He held out his hand. "I'm Dave Allison."

"Walt Staley." He liked Allison's handshake and the way his gray eyes met his own. He said: "I figured to spend the night here."

"Glad to have you," Allison said, motioning to one of the soldiers. "Staley, meet Johnny Morgan. He's my bunky."

"Howdy, Mister Staley." Morgan came forward eagerly, hand extended.

This one was big, as tall as Allison and much heavier, but he bulged in the wrong places. He's all blubber, Staley thought, and then he realized the soldier was young, hardly more than a boy. He might have muscles under that baby fat.

Staley shook hands with three others who moved forward indifferently—ordinary, run-of-the-mill soldiers who likely had joined the Army so they would not have to worry about where their next meal came from. Allison called them Al Cady, Ben Plunkett, and Nelse Luckel. They might as well have been Tom, Dick, and Harry. But Allison was different. So was the man sitting with his back to the wall.

"Put your horse in the corral," Allison said. "You can mess with us. We can't offer you much of a menu, but we've got plenty of what there is."

"Ain't you gonna introduce your new friend to me?" the sitting man asked.

He didn't look up. He didn't miss a stroke with his knife. Long feathery splinters floated to the ground. He had good muscle control, and Staley could not miss the hostility in his tone. This one was trouble.

Johnny Morgan looked scared. Cady, Plunkett,

and Luckel wore sly grins, as if they expected a bit of entertainment.

"Well, Pete," Allison said coolly, "I didn't see any sense in introducing you. You're never interested in anybody but yourself."

The whittler laughed as he stood up and tossed away the stick. "Now that ain't rightly true, Dave, and you know it. I'm interested in Madame Fifi's girls, especially that purty little Christine. . . . Oh, I'm sorry, Johnny. I keep forgetting how mushy you are about her. But, hell, I can't help it if she likes me."

Johnny Morgan's face turned red. A pulse started to pound in his forehead. But he didn't move. Staley glanced at Morgan, then at Pete, and decided that the fellow was a fighter as well as a bully. He was of only average height, but he had wide shoulders and thick arms, with a bullet head atop a short, corded neck. His face gave him away: cauliflower ears, flat nose, scars around his eyes and mouth, all the marks of dozens of fights that he had probably won because hitting him would be like slamming a fist into the wall of a house.

"All right, Pete," Allison said. "I'll introduce you. Pete Risdon, meet Walt Staley."

Risdon held his pocket knife in his right hand, the long blade open. His pale blue eyes raked Staley's tall body, from his battered hat with the Sioux bullet hole in the crown, then down his buckskin shirt and pants to his beaded moccasins.

"Howdy, Staley," Risdon said with cold insolence. "You look like one of them plainsmen we hear about."

"You might call me that," Staley agreed. "You look like one of Uncle Sam's soldiers who's been eating hardtack so long his gut's turned into one long, hard pipe."

Risdon laughed delightedly. "That's about it, mister. I've always wondered about you plainsmen. You been living with the Indians this winter?"

"That's right," Staley said. "I wintered with the Crows."

"Let him alone, Pete," Allison said. "He just got here. He'll be riding along in the morning."

"Maybe he'll be riding along tonight," Risdon said. "I don't like plainsmen. They ruin the Indians. Live with 'em. Sleep with 'em. Eat with 'em. Make the redskins think they're as good as we are."

"Let him alone," Allison said. "He's staying tonight. You're not running him off."

Staley saw that this was between Risdon and Allison, a feud of long standing that had never come to a showdown. He watched Risdon turn his head just enough to look at Allison, caught the calculating glint in his pale eyes, and sensed that Risdon wasn't at all sure he could take Allison. Not being sure, he hadn't pushed the feud to a finish.

"Well, now, Dave," Risdon said, "maybe we'd

better let the corporal decide whether he stays or not." Slowly Risdon's head turned on his great neck until his gaze raked Staley again. "So you lived with the Crows. Had a squaw keep you warm all winter, huh?"

"He did better than you did," Allison said. "I didn't see any squaws keeping you warm."

Risdon grinned. "Now that ain't right, Dave boy. I could have got a squaw, but, hell, they stink. Of course a feller like Staley here wouldn't notice 'cause he stinks so bad he couldn't smell the squaw."

Staley let out a yell that sounded like an Indian war whoop. He lunged at Risdon, yanking his knife from his scabbard before he completed his first step. He held it in front of him, hand weaving, sunlight glittering on the bright steel.

Risdon back pedaled. He dropped his pocket knife, stumbled over a chunk of dirt, and sprawled flat on his back. Staley dropped on him. His knees slammed into Risdon's belly, driving the wind out of his lungs in a wheezy sigh.

Staley's knife point pressed against Risdon's throat hard enough to draw a trickle of blood. A man ran toward them from the stable, shouting: "Don't do it! Don't do it! Stop him somebody! Allison, stop him!"

But neither Allison nor anybody else moved to stop Staley. Blood trickled down Risdon's neck. He froze, his eyes bulging from their sockets.

"I was aiming to gut him," Staley said, "but maybe cutting his throat would be better."

"No use dirtying up your knife, is there, Staley?" Allison asked.

The man from the stable tugged at Staley's shoulder.

"I'm Corporal Jones," he said. "Corporal Jones. Don't kill him. Don't kill him, I say."

Staley rose and stepped to one side. "I didn't see you come up, Corporal. I was busy with this leftover buffalo chip. What's he good for?"

"He's a good soldier," Jones said. "He's a good soldier."

Risdon sat up, feeling his throat. He looked at his fingers and saw blood. "You bastard, you were going to kill me, weren't you?"

"I will yet if you don't learn to keep a civil tongue in your head," Staley said.

"You know, Pete," Allison said, "that was the nearest you'll ever come to getting your throat cut until someone really does it."

Risdon rubbed his neck and measured Staley carefully.

"Put your knife up, Staley. I'll fight you with my fists."

"Oh no, you won't," Staley said. "We ain't kids having a brawl at recess back of the schoolhouse. If you want another go at me, pick up your knife." He motioned to the pocket knife Risdon had dropped. "We'll finish it right now.

Unexpectedly Risdon grinned. "Uhn-uh," he grunted. "I'm satisfied to leave it lay this way. I'll take care of your horse."

He picked up his knife, closed the blade, and shoved the knife deep into his pocket. Then he took the buckskin's reins and led him toward the stable.

"Is this how you make friends in the Army?" Staley asked Allison.

"It's the way you make friends with Pete Risdon," Allison said sourly. "If you can whip him, you're his friend. If you can't, he rubs your nose into the dirt."

"What was it about?" the corporal demanded. "You can't just ride in here and half kill one of my men. . . ."

"I came in here to stay the night and do you a favor," Staley said. "I'll do more than half kill anybody who acts like that bastard."

Jones stood half a head shorter than Staley and was by far the oldest of the seven soldiers in the hay camp. He was a roly-poly man, but he didn't give the impression of being soft. Staley figured him to be a career soldier who had joined the service before the Civil War and would stay in until he retired.

"All right," Jones said. "What's the favor?"

"Are your horses in?" Staley asked.

"No. We didn't need them today, so we turned them out to graze."

"Then get 'em in," Staley said. "There's Indians all over the country. They'll have 'em before morning if you leave 'em out."

"Aw, what kind of bull are you giving us?" Al Cady asked. "We've been here most of the winter and we ain't seen no Indians."

Jones nodded agreement. "They wouldn't come this close to Fort Laramie, mister. I've fought Indians from here to the Río Grande and I can smell 'em if they're anywhere around."

"Then you've got a damned poor smeller," Staley said. "I had dinner at Barrone's horse ranch and he told me there was a dozen bands drifting through the country. I've only run across the tracks of one band, but that was only a few miles east of here. I judged there were eight braves in the party."

Jones scratched a bronze cheek, his eyes thoughtful. "All right, we'll run 'em in."

"Come on inside, Staley," Allison said. "I'm the cook tonight."

"I don't trust our friend Risdon," Staley said. "I'm going to see how well he's taking care of my horse."

"I've got a couple of minutes," Allison said. "I'll walk to the stable with you. But I think you'll be surprised. Risdon is a good hand with horses."

When they were a dozen steps from the others, Staley said in a low tone: "Looks to me like Risdon has got this outfit buffaloed."

"Yes, I guess he has," Allison agreed gravely. "I'm glad you handled him the way you did. I never saw him down before."

"Have you tangled with him?"

"No."

"It'll come," Staley said.

"Yeah, it'll come." Allison sighed. "If we live long enough. I'm not looking forward to it."

Staley nodded, knowing how men like Risdon fought. He would butt, elbow, and kick. He would even gouge eyes out if he got his man down. Allison would be lucky if he wasn't maimed for life.

CHAPTER FIVE

As soon as Staley finished eating, he picked up his Winchester and went to the door.

"You soldier boys get a good night's sleep in your bunks," he said. "Maybe it don't make any difference whether you lose your horses or not, but I can't afford to lose my buckskin."

"If the Indians show up," Corporal Jones said, "just holler. We'll be there to give you a hand."

"I'll watch for you," Staley said. "I'll watch till my eyes bug out."

He stepped outside and walked to the stable. The evening was warmer than a man had a right to expect at this time of year. Tomorrow it might snow, but it was still spring tonight. He leaned his Winchester against the wall of the stable, then looked in on his buckskin. Allison had been right about the way Risdon took care of a horse. The man had spent more time on the buckskin than a hostler in a livery stable would. Stranger still, he acted as if he enjoyed doing it.

"This is a hell of a good animal," Risdon had said. "I wish I owned him."

"I don't aim to sell him," Staley had said. "He's carried me a lot of miles and he'll carry me some more. After a while you get to thinking a horse like this is your friend."

Risdon had nodded thoughtfully, his knobby, scarred face turning bleak. "He's a gelding, so you can depend on him. Same thing with a stallion. But you can't count on a mare. Fact is, you can't count on any female."

Risdon had walked out of the stable then, fists knotted at his sides. *Some woman had sold him out,* Staley thought. *Maybe his wife had run off with another man.* Staley had no figures to prove it, but he suspected that unfaithful women caused more men to join the Army than any other reason.

Staley carried his saddle and blanket out of the stable and dropped them near the door. He sat down and filled and lighted his pipe. Some of the soldiers drifted out of the bunkhouse. Allison was the only one who came to the stable, which suited Staley just fine.

Allison hunkered beside Staley and filled his pipe. When he had it going, he said: "Ready for the Indians?"

After a pause in which he decided Allison was sincere in asking the question, Staley said: "As ready as I'll ever be. The fact is, you're never really ready for an Indian. He's too tricky. Before daylight I'll hear some coyotes out yonder and the chances are I won't know whether they're Indians or coyotes."

"You must like Indians," Allison said, "or you wouldn't live with them."

"You live with white soldiers," Staley said. "Does that prove you like all of 'em?"

Allison took the pipe out of his mouth and laughed.

"My guess is, you don't like any of the men you're living with," Staley said.

"That's taking in too much territory," Allison said. "I like Johnny Morgan. Or maybe I feel sorry for him. He's the kind you have to look out for."

"Well, redskins are like whites," Staley said. "You cotton to some of 'em and others are pure poison. Sure, Indians are superstitious and ignorant and in a lot of ways they're so damned cruel it makes you sick. But in other ways they're a brave, freedom-loving, independent kind of people and I respect that."

"That makes sense," Allison admitted.

"There's one part of this quarrel the white man has with the Indian that I don't savvy," Staley said. "Uncle Sam makes a treaty with some tribe like the Sioux. The treaty says the Sioux can keep a certain piece of land. The Black Hills, for instance. The Sioux ride home after the palaver, aiming to keep the treaty and be peaceful, but then something happens.

"A white man sneaks into the Black Hills and finds gold. He tells other white men and pretty soon you've got ten thousand people on Indian land that was supposed to be theirs forever. So then Uncle Sam works it around until we have a war going. The Indians get in a few licks, but in the end they lose.

"Then the Sioux have to sign a new treaty that gives the Black Hills to Uncle Sam. And Uncle Sam says to the ten thousand people who broke the law by going onto Indian land that it's all legal now. He says they can stay and keep on digging the gold they've been digging all this time. You tell me who's civilized and who's a savage."

"You sound bitter," Allison said.

"It's just that I know the Indian side of the row," Staley said. "But that won't help me one damned bit if the Cheyennes who are sashaying through the country get their hands on me. I'll die slow and full of pain."

"If the Indian is bound to lose in the end," Allison said thoughtfully, "why can't he see it?"

"Some of them do," Staley said. "The point is, they'd rather die fighting than get kicked in the butt all the time. The average Indian won't die fighting, though. He'll get beaten because he's starved and he'll wind up being put on a reservation that's the worst land in the country. That's where he'll stay till the white man finds gold on that worst land . . . and then he'll get shoved off regardless of how many sacred treaties have been signed. Aw, hell, Allison, sometimes it makes me ashamed of being a white man."

Allison knocked his pipe against his heel and

filled it again. Night had moved across the prairie, and here and there stars were beginning to show in a steadily darkening sky. He lighted his pipe and asked: "Were you raised out here in the West?"

"Yeah, except for the first ten years of my life. My folks lived in Ohio, I came out to Denver with 'em in 'Fifty-Nine. They died from typhoid fever the next year. Since then I've made it by myself. Of course, there's been times when I've gone mighty hungry."

Allison nodded, pulling on his pipe.

"I guess men join the Army for all kinds of reasons," Staley said. "What about Risdon? He ever tell you where he came from and why he joined up?"

"He doesn't talk much about himself," Allison said. "He's been in the Army two years. I think he came from Chicago, but I'm not sure. It's the only city he's ever mentioned."

Staley told Allison about Risdon's remarks concerning females.

"It ain't the way most men feel," he added. "I mean, a lot of us get kicked in the teeth by a woman, but we get over it. He hasn't. He's bitter. I got a notion he hates all women."

"I never heard him say he did," Allison said thoughtfully. "But every time we go to the hog ranch he gets ornery. I pity any girl who goes to bed with him. She earns her money."

They sat in silence for a time, smoking. Then

Allison said: "You going to the fort tomorrow?"

"I figured on it," Staley said, "though I ain't real anxious to make the ride alone. I didn't much more than miss that Cheyenne band yesterday. I hate to push my luck."

"Johnny and I are taking a load of hay to the fort tomorrow," Allison said. "You'd better ride with us."

"I'd sure like to," Staley said. "Three rifles beat one."

"We'll be in a hell of a fix if they attack us here," Allison said.

"Only if they catch you out loading up hay and you're scattered," Staley said. "Unless it's a big band, they won't give you any trouble except to burn your haystacks or steal your horses."

"The trouble is, we're almost out of ammunition," Allison said. "I was out here last summer and I helped put up the hay and build these buildings. Then they ordered me back to the fort for the winter months so I could be the post schoolteacher. I just got back here the First of April. Sometime while I was gone, the men shot up most of the ammunition and the corporal hasn't asked for more."

"Then he's a fool," Staley said.

"You may be right at that," Allison said, and sighed. "They wasted the ammunition on jack rabbits and antelopes, but they never saw any Indians. So now it's a proposition of Jones having to own up that he let them waste the ammunition. He can't lie about being attacked by the Indians and make it stick."

"Something is sure as hell going to stick if you get pinned down here without any ammunition," Staley said.

Allison rose and knocked the ashes from his pipe. "Guess I'd better roll in. We're working tomorrow. Today was an off day." He slipped the pipe into his pocket, then he said: "You were asking about Risdon. None of us has figured him out. He got into so much trouble on straight line duty that they made a bedpan pusher out of him. Then one night he drank the whiskey he was supposed to be doling out to a patient, so the next stop was the guardhouse. When he got out, they put him on detached service, loading hay. Now we're stuck with him."

"He must hate everything and everybody," Staley said, "or he wouldn't be on the prod like he is."

"He has only contempt for a man he can whip," Allison said, "but if he gets whipped, he thinks the man who did it is great. That doesn't happen often. But he doesn't hate everything. He loves animals, males anyway. He showed that with a dog we had at the fort. It's the same with horses."

"Sometimes I think a man is almost as much of a mystery as a woman," Staley said.

"Almost," Allison agreed. "Almost."

He walked away, leaving Staley to wonder if some woman was responsible for Dave Allison's being in the Army.

Staley finished his pipe and lay down, his head on his saddle, the blanket pulled over him. The talk with Allison had stirred old memories. Ordinarily he was not a man to dwell on the past, but now, once again, he lived through that hot night in Denver. It had been so long ago, but he could still hear his fever-stricken parents groaning and rolling in the rickety bed. Before the night ended, typhoid had burned their lives out of them.

He remembered how helpless he had felt, and he remembered the funeral and the preacher's futile effort to comfort him. After that, the memories blurred until he was sixteen and big enough to draw man wages on a ranch.

No, he didn't want to think about the five years in between, years of beatings and abuse and being kicked from one home to another. He'd done his share of hating in those days. If he hadn't taken up with an old trapper in South Park, he might have turned out to be another Pete Risdon.

The trapper's name was Jake Dice. With Jake, Staley had learned the wilderness. He and Jake had tramped all over the Colorado Rockies. They had even lived for a time with the Utes. He got over his hating during those years because Jake didn't hate anything or anybody.

"You just make yourself sick if you hate," the old man used to say. "Hate's a slow poison."

It was true. Staley had seen it work time after time. It was working now with Pete Risdon. Risdon was a sick man.

Staley had been able to accept Jake's death without bitterness. Jake was old and crippled up with rheumatism. It was time for him to die and he knew it. After that, Staley drifted around all over Colorado and Wyoming. He'd had some bad times and some good ones, but of all the good ones, Sir Cedric Smith's hunting trip was the best.

Staley had been the Englishman's guide, and a Denver reporter named Patrick O'Hara had ridden with the party. Staley had liked O'Hara from the first, and because Sir Cedric believed in sharing his own good fortune at every stop along the trail, they had lived high on the hog. When it was over, Smith had gone back to England with his trophies, O'Hara took a job with the *Cheyenne Leader*, and Staley felt as if he had just moved out of paradise.

The big money he had earned that summer slipped through his fingers. He had lived his shiftless years. Now he had nothing, and he wanted to marry Tally Barrone. Well, he'd always found a way and he'd find it this time. He went to sleep at last with that comforting thought in his mind.

CHAPTER SIX

Staley had just finished his second cup of breakfast coffee when Johnny Morgan, who was standing in the doorway rolling a cigarette, let out a scared yell. For a moment the other soldiers just stared at him. Staley was off the bench and halfway to the door before anybody else made a move. He grabbed his Winchester and ran outside.

A man in a wagon was racing his horses toward the hay camp. A band of Indians was gaining on him. There were eight of them, or nine. Staley couldn't be sure in that first quick glance.

They were strung out for fifty yards behind the driver, but two braves were well ahead of the rest and coming up fast on opposite sides of the teamster. One had a rifle in his hands, the other a lance ready to sink into the teamster's back.

Staley dropped to one knee and eared back the hammer of his rifle. It was a long shot, so long that luck more than skill would determine whether he scored a hit or not. In any case, he could not get both lead Indians in time to save the man's life.

Staley took careful aim, then squeezed off the shot. The brave with the rifle threw up his arms and went off the horse in a rolling fall. In that same instant the other Indian drove his lance into the teamster's back. He fell forward off his seat,

45

the horses coming straight on toward the hay camp in a hard run.

Staley emptied the Winchester, but he missed every shot. The Indians picked up the fallen brave, wheeled, and raced away. Staley stood up and filled his magazine.

"Have you got any saddles?" he called to Jones.

"Three old McClellans," the corporal snapped. "But you ain't leading any of my men out there to get killed." He wheeled to face the men who stood behind him. "Cady, you and Plunkett fetch in that wagon. We'll see if the teamster's dead."

Staley waited until Jones turned back, then said: "Have you got enough ammunition to fight off an attack?"

"No," Jones said. "We sure as hell don't."

"Give me three men on horses and we'll chase 'em a while," Staley said. "They won't stand and fight, and they won't bother you for a spell if we give 'em a run. If we don't, they'll hang around and try to pick off some of your boys. Now how about it?"

Jones scratched the back of his neck, scowling doubtfully. Then he nodded. "All right, if you can get three of 'em to go with you."

"I'll go," Allison said. "Come on, Johnny. We might as well get in on the fun."

Morgan held back, glancing at Staley, then at Jones, and finally at Allison. He gulped and said: "All right, I'll go."

46

"You two saddle up," Staley said. "I need one more."

The rest shifted their weight from one foot to another. They stared at the ground or across the prairie as if wanting suddenly to become invisible. Then Pete Risdon laughed.

"Well, you only live once," he said. "Let's go."

"Get 'em back here by noon," Jones said to Staley. "Allison and Morgan are taking a load of hay to the fort this afternoon."

"If we don't jump the Indians and throw a little lead," Staley said, "the chances are you won't get that load halfway to the fort."

He ran to the corral and saddled his buckskin. Five minutes later they rode east.

Young Morgan looked as if he was sorry he'd agreed to go. By the time they had ridden half a mile Staley was sorry he'd let the boy come. Morgan rode like a sack of wool, weaving from side to side in the saddle. He had all he could do to hold the reins in one hand, the rifle in the other, and keep his butt against leather. Staley had to motion repeatedly for him to move up.

The trail angled northeast. When they stopped at a creek to water their horses, Allison said: "You act like you want to find the bastards."

"I do," Staley said. "Too many bands are running around looking for horses and easy scalps with nobody bothering 'em. They need to hear a few bullets whistle past their ears. That lucky shot I got in back there at the hay camp did more good than anything that's happened lately."

"I'm going back," Johnny Morgan said.

"All right," Staley said. "But have you ever seen a man who's been scalped?"

Morgan blinked at him. "They're still a long ways ahead of us . . . ain't they?"

"You think so?" Staley laughed softly. "Go ahead, boy. Start back." He looked at Allison. "Have you got the name and address of his folks? They'll want to know."

Allison nodded. "I'll write to them."

Staley stepped into the saddle and put his buckskin up the steep north bank. He turned east when he came out of the box elders that flanked the stream, following Indian tracks toward the Barrone Ranch. Morgan kept up better than before, but all three soldiers were mounted on work horses and even Allison, who seemed to be a good rider, was having trouble holding the pace that Staley set.

About the middle of the morning they climbed a steep hill. Reaching the top, they saw a herd of fifty or more horses headed up the valley. The Indians were behind them, pushing the animals as hard as they could.

"We got 'em!" Staley yelled in triumph. "Dismount and fight on foot the way the cavalry does."

He swung down and dropped on his belly in the

grass. The Indians started up the hill toward them, but when Staley began shooting, they wheeled their ponies and raced toward the brush along the banks of the stream that meandered across the floor of the valley.

Staley emptied his Winchester, hitting one brave. Allison and Risdon got in three shots apiece before the curtain of brush closed behind the Indians. But Morgan, who lay motionless beside Allison, hadn't fired a shot.

Staley rose and reloaded. He said: "You better learn to pull that trigger, kid. You don't turn Indians back by staring at 'em."

"I ain't a very good shot," Morgan mumbled. "I figured I'd better save my ammunition."

Staley shook his head. "These boys didn't have the belly for a real fight, but if they had, four rifles talking instead of three would have been a good argument to change their minds."

Allison and Risdon came to their feet. "We gonna chase 'em any more?" Risdon asked.

"Nope. It'd be suicide to ride into that brush yonder. They'd cut us down before we got halfway there." Staley motioned to the horses. "We'll round up these animals and head 'em for Barrone's ranch. They must be his. He's got the only spread within twenty miles of here."

"I guess I figured you wrong," Risdon said. "I've seen a lot of half-breeds and white men that wore buckskin, fellers that had lived most of their lives amongst the Indians. Most of 'em were a lot of wind, but you don't seem to be that kind."

"Seem to?" Allison laughed. "Eight redskins come heading for us, and Staley says . . . 'We've got 'em!'"

Staley shrugged. "I figured this bunch was looking for horses more than scalps. They ain't likely to bother you now."

He glanced at Morgan, who stood beside his horse, one hand on his saddle, his face so white that Staley wouldn't have been surprised if he'd fainted and fallen to the ground. He added: "That's why it's a good idea to fire a few times in a deal like this whether you hit anything or not. Most Indians don't pick a fight unless the odds are running in their favor. They could have figured odds of eight to three favored 'em enough to come after us . . . but eight to four might have looked different."

Morgan understood him. "They could see we had four horses," he said huskily.

"But they didn't know four horses had four riders who had four rifles." Staley turned to his buckskin, not wanting to waste time arguing with a scared boy like Morgan. Either he grew up enough to do his share of the fighting, or in the end he'd run and probably die a coward.

"Let's get those horses rounded up," Staley said.

As he mounted, he wondered why Johnny Morgan had joined the Army.

50

CHAPTER SEVEN

Staley told Risdon and Morgan to ride along the crest of the ridge so they could get around the horse herd without spooking them. He'd ride more slowly with Allison and hold the horses between the creek and the ridge. He was afraid they would scatter in all directions when the two soldiers started driving them back down the valley.

He knew it would be a tricky job to round up the horses and still stay far enough from the creek to remain out of rifle range of the Indians. He had warned Risdon and Morgan not to get too close to the brush. It was not as thick opposite the horses as it was here, but it might be dense enough to hide an Indian sharpshooter.

Staley hadn't seen any of the braves ride out of the brush on the far side. He didn't think they would as long as there was a chance that a white man might make the mistake of getting too close to one of them.

A moment later he glanced back and saw three riders appear over the crest of the ridge. They were too far away to identify, but they didn't figure to be Indians. The Indians did their raiding in larger parties, and if three scouts spotted a larger bunch of white men, they didn't keep on coming. They rode away and the whole party hit you later.

No, those three must be Louis Barrone and his sons out looking for horses. If the Indians hiding in the brush were Cheyennes, they wouldn't shoot the Barrone boys, and they probably wouldn't hurt Louie. If Tally was right, his time would come later. In any case, the problem of recovering the horses belonged to the Barrones, not Staley and the three soldiers who were supposed to be back at the hay camp by noon.

Staley yelled to Allison to turn back and to tell Risdon and Morgan. Allison nodded and shouted at the other two.

As Staley reined toward the approaching riders, he lifted his hat, the Chinook sign of a white man. By the time Allison, Risdon, and Morgan joined him, Staley had recognized Louie Barrone and his sons.

When they came within shouting distance, Barrone bellowed: "It's a good thing you lifted your hat or we'd have let you have it! We figured you was the red devils that had run our horses off!"

"It wouldn't have been gratitude to shoot us," Staley said. "We're the ones who stopped the Indians from running your horses off. They're still down there along the creek."

"The hell." Barrone's gaze swept the brush. Then he glanced at his boys as if mentally measuring the risk in going after his horses. "I reckon they won't try to take 'em away from us."

He looked at the soldiers. "How'd you get the cavalry out?"

"These men are mounted infantry," Staley said, and introduced them.

Barrone said: "Howdy." His voice was friendly, but his sons gave the soldiers surly, half-inch nods, their dark eyes hostile. The old man sensed their attitude, Staley thought, because he growled something about fetching the horses in, and then turned his back to them as they rode off.

"We'd better head back to camp," Allison said. "The corporal will have our hides if we don't get that load of hay to the fort this afternoon."

As Staley watched the Barrone boys gallop away, it occurred to him that he would never have a better time to talk to the old man about marrying Tally.

"Go ahead," he told Allison. "I'll catch up. I want to talk to Louie."

Allison grinned. "I guess your buckskin can move faster than these plugs we're on." He winked at Barrone. "I'm afraid the cavalry would be disgraced for life if they had to ride horses like these."

"I reckon so." Barrone grinned back as he scratched his nose. After the soldiers had ridden away, he said: "I like that one. I've scouted for the Army ever since they laid the chunk, and most of the time I wonder how they ever win a scrap with the Injuns, considering the men they use.

Take that fat young 'un. He's all blubber. Ain't good for nothing. The older man's a tough if I ever seen one. Ain't got a brain in that bullet head of his. But that tall boy looks like he oughta be an officer."

"I've wondered why he ain't," Staley said. "Allison, that's the tall one, he's officer material, all right, but he's the kind who thinks for himself. Chances are he's spent half his time in the guardhouse for doing it."

"He won't stay in the Army," Barrone said. "What'd you want to talk to me about, Walt?"

"Well, I didn't have much chance yesterday to talk." Staley moistened his lips, almost losing his nerve, then plunged on: "I want to marry Tally, Louie. Of course we hope it's all right with you."

Barrone stared at Staley, his leathery old face turning hard, his eyes narrowing. He said: "If I didn't know you as well as I do, Walt, I'd think living with the Crows all winter made you lose whatever sense you was born with. Maybe that's what happened. Wintering with the Crows is enough to turn even a smart man into an idiot."

Staley's first reaction was one of anger so complete that he had to fight an impulse to pull the old man out of his saddle and break his neck. A good part of a minute passed before he trusted himself to say: "I don't take that kindly, Louie."

"What the hell did you expect me to say?"

54

Barrone asked harshly. "It won't do. I thought you had sense enough to know it."

"I don't have any money, if that's what's eating on you," Staley said, "but I'll look after her. I can tell you one thing. She'll have a better life with me than you've given her so far, and a whole lot better than she'll have in the future if she stays with you."

"What're you talking about?"

"I'm saying that the day will come when you can't handle your sons the way you always have. When it does, they'll ride out and take Tally with 'em. And then they'll give her to some Cheyenne buck whether she likes it or not."

"I'll handle 'em," Barrone said. "I'll never see the day I can't handle 'em. If they do ride out, they won't take Tally with 'em. You can count on that."

"Either way, you can't keep a girl like Tally with you forever. What's your objection to me as a son-in-law?"

"Nothing," Barrone said, " 'cept you're white. It won't work. I thought you had been around 'breeds enough to know that."

"It worked for you with a full-blood," Staley said. "Why wouldn't it work for me?"

"It didn't work for me and you know it as well as I do," Barrone said hotly. "I tell you the whites won't have nothing to do with Tally and the Injuns won't want her, either, unless she goes Injun. Is that what you're figuring to do?"

"No," Staley said. "I'll take her away from this country. I'll make a good home for her."

"She's still a half-breed," the old man said passionately. "You ain't smart enough to change that. Your kids will be half-breeds, too, and the door will be closed to 'em anywhere they go. My boys can't even go to a stinkin' hog ranch. I told Madame Fifi they wanted to do business there and she cussed me like a muleskinner. She says . . . 'You think I'm runnin' this place for fun? If I let 'em come, I'll lose all my business.' That's the way it is everywhere."

"You're stubborn, Louie," Staley said. "Too stubborn to see what's going to happen to her if she stays with you."

Barrone stroked his beard, his hard eyes fixed on Staley. Then he said: "Stay away from her, Walt. I'll shoot you if you come sneaking around trying to see her."

He galloped past Staley toward the horses that were being herded down the valley. Staley reined over the ridge top and rode down the steep slope, telling himself he would go after Tally today if he had any money. But he didn't. He'd need at least a month, and then he'd come back after her if he had to fight both Louie and his boys. All he could do now was hope she'd be all right until then.

CHAPTER EIGHT

Staley rode alongside the wagon from the hay camp to Fort Laramie that afternoon, and he sensed that both Allison and Morgan were scared. Allison kept his fear under control, but Morgan was so nervous that every time he spoke his voice shook.

Staley knew the Indians might still be in the area, and if they were, three men with a good buckskin saddle horse and team would be worth attacking. He didn't mention this, partly because he knew Morgan could not stand a heavier burden of fear, and partly because he had never been a man to expect the worst to happen.

Halfway to the fort, Allison pointed to a two-story, unpainted house that had been built since Staley had traveled this road. A woodshed and privy stood behind it, with an adobe corral and slab shed a little farther down the road.

"That's the hog ranch we were talking about," Allison said. "The madam calls herself Fifi, but she sounds more like Mary Jones or Susy Smith from Ohio."

"You ought to see her niece," Morgan said. "Her name's Christine. She sure is a beaut'."

"She's not the kind you'd expect to find in a place like that," Allison agreed. "She's not one of the working girls. All Fifi lets her do is serve drinks and wait on tables."

"She's crazy to build so far from the fort," Staley said. "Does she figure her girls are Indian fighters?"

Allison laughed. "That's not what she hired them for, but she claims all of them can shoot. She's got just one man working for her, a big Negro named Nero. She built strong, with double walls and shutters for the windows and bars for the doors."

"Has she got plenty of rifles and ammunition?" Staley asked.

"She says so," Allison said. "I've seen her rifles. She keeps them on racks near the back and front doors. As for being closer to the fort, she said she'd get enough soldier trade out here, and she wanted to be far enough away so the cowboys and freighters wouldn't think she was only catering to soldiers. She's a smart old hag. When the Indian trouble is over, the government will close the fort and move the soldiers, but the cowboys and freighters will be here a long time."

"She'll be here a real long time if the Sioux decide to burn her out," Staley said. "She'll be six feet under."

Allison shrugged. "She's not a woman to worry. The Indians were quiet when she built the place, but even if they'd been on the prod, she'd have built anyway."

"She promised Christine she could take over as

madam when she retires," Morgan said. "We think Christine is her daughter, not her niece."

"You mean *you* think so, Johnny," Allison said. "I don't. And I don't think Christine wants to be a madam, either. All she wants is to get out of the damned place and I don't think Fifi is going to let her go. She's not only smart, she's mean."

"She don't mistreat Christine," Morgan said. "She's good to her."

Allison just chuckled.

An hour later they reached the fort. Allison said he and Morgan would pick up mail, unload the hay behind the stables, and then head back to camp. It would be late when they arrived, but there was less chance of meeting Indians at night.

"I hope I run into you boys again," Staley said. "If I can talk Crook into giving me a job, I probably will."

"He needs scouts," Allison said. He hesitated as if he had something to add, then shrugged. "Good luck, Staley."

"Good luck to you," Staley said, and rode toward Crook's headquarters.

A wind had sprung up, and as Staley crossed the parade ground, he heard the halyards slap sharply against the flagpole. He dismounted, glancing westward. A mass of black clouds was rolling into the sky, promising a spring storm. Well, this time he wouldn't be out in it.

Staley had never met General Crook, but he

knew men who had served under Crook and they liked and respected him. In appearance, Crook certainly lived up to his reputation. He was in his late forties, an athletic-appearing man without an ounce of surplus flesh on his lean body. He wore his light brown hair close-cropped, and his blond beard parted at the point of his chin. Staley particularly liked the way Crook's blue-gray eyes met his, and the general's strong grip when they shook hands.

"Glad you came in," Crook said. "I've heard of you and I do need help."

"I'm after a job, all right," Staley said, "but there's some things I ought to tell you first."

"Go ahead."

Staley brought him up to date in regard to Indian affairs around the Barrone Ranch and the Army hay camp.

"Well," Crook said, "I can't send a detail out to chase Indians every time they steal horses. It's like putting your finger on a flea. You see the flea, all right, but by the time your hand gets there, he's gone."

Staley just nodded. He had expected Crook to say exactly that, flea included.

"One more thing," Staley said. "The soldiers at the hay camp are almost out of ammunition."

"Why?" Crook snapped. "Some of them come to the fort every day or so. What's the matter with them?"

"It's like this," Staley said. "They had plenty of ammunition when the hay camp was built, but they shot most of it away on rabbits and antelopes. I guess Corporal Jones was embarrassed to ask for more."

Crook was plainly irritated. He motioned to his orderly. "See that one hundred rounds per man are sent to the hay camp with the wagon that just came in."

The orderly saluted and left. Crook leaned back in his chair and studied Staley. Finally, he said: "What kind of job did you want?"

"I ain't particular," Staley answered, "as long as it ain't dull and pays good money."

"I need a man who knows the country and knows Indians. A man who can eat berries in order to survive, and then tell me the truth about what he's seen when he returns. I want a man who avoids unnecessary fighting, but can fight if he has to. As I've already said, I know you by reputation. Louie Barrone speaks highly of you. I believe you'll fill the bill, and I can promise that the job will not be dull. It will be dangerous."

"The pay?" Staley asked.

Crook held up his hand. "Let me tell you about the job first. I want a messenger to carry dispatches to other forts and other commands. Plans are being made for an extensive campaign this summer, probably beginning next month. The country will be alive with Indians, so it will be necessary to ride by night and sleep in the daytime."

"The pay?" Staley asked again.

Crook pretended he didn't hear. "Right now the wires are down between here and Fetterman. I have dispatches to send. You will leave as soon as you have your supper."

Staley took a long breath. He suspected that Crook was baiting him. Patience was a basic virtue when it came to working your way through Indian country. If he blew up now, Crook would say he was not the man for the job.

"General," he said, "I'm prepared to carry your dispatches through every Indian tribe between here and hell . . . if the pay is worth it."

Crook smiled. "The pay is one hundred twenty-five per month if we furnish your horse, or one fifty if you have a horse."

"I have the horse," Staley said.

"All right," Crook said. "Be back here within an hour."

The sun was almost down when Staley left Fort Laramie. He was going to be out in the storm after all. The air was cold and damp, and lightning kept playing all along the western horizon. He would be wet long before he reached Fetterman, but at $150 a month he could afford to get wet.

CHAPTER NINE

Dave Allison and Johnny Morgan unloaded hay, picked up mail, and headed out of Fort Laramie. The forbidding darkness of the sky guaranteed that the storm would hit them long before they reached the hay camp.

They probably could reach the hog ranch, but Madame Fifi did not favor soldiers who used her place as a haven to escape a storm. She was there for business, not conversation.

Allison was a better hand with horses than Morgan, but this team was gentle enough for Morgan to handle. Allison hadn't looked at the mail, so he handed the lines to Morgan and went through the contents of the mail sack. Most of it was impersonal: newspapers, magazines, and a package from Corporal Jones's wife, who lived in Cheyenne. Among the half dozen letters Allison found one from his father.

"Anything for me?" Morgan asked.

"Not a thing, Johnny."

Morgan sighed. "I had a letter from Mom last week. I probably won't get another one till next week." He sighed again. "I dunno why I ever joined up, Dave. I could be home with one of Mom's good suppers in me and no Indian in five hundred miles."

Allison only half heard. He stared ahead at the twin ruts running through the sagebrush.

He had known for a long time that he couldn't go home. He loved his father but he could not face his neighbors, or Franny Knowles's aunt and uncle, or even Franny herself if she ever came back. Foolish pride, perhaps, but that's the way it was.

His mother had died when he was ten years old and his father had raised him. His father had done a good job, considering the fact that he was forty years old when Allison was born and had never been around children.

Allison's father had a small farm that gave them vegetables and meat. He preached every Sunday at a nearby country church, and that gave him a few dollars. He usually had more vegetables than dollars.

Somehow his father had never understood the world outside, the world of violence and brutality and wickedness. Perhaps he did not even know this world existed. He loved his neighbors. Most of them belonged to his church.

Few strangers came into his community and he seldom left it. Neighbors helped each other, and Dave Allison, growing up in this rural community where nothing ever seemed to change, thought that was the way people were.

He'd gone as far in school as he could while staying at home, and he had no money to go away.

He helped his father on the farm, and he spent much time reading. His father owned many books: classics and history and biography as well as religious tomes. Allison read them all, then borrowed every book he heard of within a ten-mile radius.

When he was twenty, two things happened that changed his life. He started to read law in Judge Croker's office in Oak Grove, the nearest town, and he fell in love with Franny Knowles, who had come to live with her aunt and uncle, Jared and Martha Knowles.

He stayed in Oak Grove during the week, sleeping on a cot in the judge's office. He walked home late Saturday afternoon, so he had Saturday evening and most of Sunday with Franny. He had never been in love before.

Franny was two years younger than Dave Allison. She was a big girl, not particularly pretty and certainly not very graceful, but she wanted a man and he needed a woman, and more than once she almost took him to bed. Because his father's attitudes had been drummed into him so thoroughly, Dave always drew back in time. And he never understood what he did to Franny.

They talked about marriage, but Dave would not give up his opportunity in the judge's office. Obviously he could not marry her and take her to Oak Grove. He assumed she would wait until he could support her, practicing law. It simply never occurred to him that Franny was becoming desperate.

He called on her one Saturday evening and Martha Knowles met him at the door. She told him that Franny had married a middle-aged widower with five children. Allison stood and stared at Mrs. Knowles for a long, long time.

Finally, he turned and walked away. He walked as long as he could, and then he sat down and cried. He considered killing himself. Then he got up and began walking again. He was simply driven to walk and walk until he reached Oak Grove. He had to get away. He could not go home. Everyone knew about him and Franny.

When the story got around, folks would laugh at him. He couldn't face them. He didn't think he could even face his father. He went into a saloon in Oak Grove and got drunk.

He stumbled out of the saloon. He passed out and spent the night in the gutter, lying in his own vomit. In the morning he was still sick. He cleaned himself up the best he could and started walking again.

When, on Monday, he staggered into Springfield and sat down to rest, the memories rushed back and filled him with despair. Then, for no reason that ever made sense to him, he joined the Army.

The Army sent him to Columbus Barracks in Ohio. He was issued the usual dark-blue blouse with its row of brass eagle buttons, two pairs of light-blue trousers, two gray flannel shirts, two suits of underwear, a light-blue wool overcoat, a pair of boots, a forage cap, a leather waist belt, and a black wool campaign hat.

His clothes didn't fit. His boots raised blisters on his feet. The underwear itched. The food was badly cooked. He had no privacy. He was assigned a bunk and a wood footlocker. The barracks had a peculiar odor, and even after he and the other recruits swabbed the floor and scrubbed the bed slats and filled the bed sacks with new straw, the odor was still there.

He drilled. He learned to march across the parade ground with his head up, stomach in, chest out, arms close to the body. He worked in fatigue details, and discovered Army discipline. He was carrying such a load of resentment that he committed one misdemeanor after another until he was fined or thrown into the guardhouse or into the bull ring, where he ran and ran, first double time and then triple time. He hated the sergeant who counted cadence while he ran. He hated the privates because they were not the kind of men he had known at home. He seemed to have nothing in common with anybody.

He welcomed being sent out to Fort D.A. Russell, where he became a part of Company A, 9th Infantry. He drank too much, and he made a reputation as a first-class brawler because the monotony of garrison life was unbearable.

It was a long time before he could bring himself to write to his father, a long time before his letters could express affection, a long time before he could force himself to ask his father to forgive him for running away.

In time he changed. He wasn't sure why. Maybe the resentment ran out. Or maybe he reached the place where he could be honest with himself and accept the fact that he had been a damned fool and had nobody to blame but himself. Or maybe some of the things Corporal Jones told him began to get through.

Whatever the reasons, he was not the same man who had joined the Army nearly three years ago. He stopped missing roll calls and being absent without leave. He began to look after Johnny Morgan, who had a talent for doing the wrong things or doing the right things wrong. Even Pete Risdon recognized him as a man who was not to be taken lightly. Maybe they would fight some-day. It didn't matter, really. He'd fought other men just as tough, and he'd learned that there was no profit in backing away from a fight.

"Dave," Morgan said.

Startled, Allison turned to Morgan, and a drop of rain hit him in the face. Lightning was slashing the sky and the rumble of thunder was closer than it had been. He took a long breath, realizing he still held his father's letter in his hand and now it was too dark to read it.

"I guess I was a long ways off," he said as he slipped the letter into his pocket. "What's on your mind, Johnny?"

"The hog ranch is over yonder," Morgan said. "What do you think?"

Suddenly Allison felt reckless. "Why not?" he said, and hoped Pete Risdon would be there. It was a good night for a fight.

CHAPTER TEN

Madame Fifi's hired man, Nero, came out of the darkness holding a lantern high. He said: "Oh, it's you, Mistuh Allison."

"And Johnny Morgan," Allison said. "Put the horses in the barn, will you?"

"You bet," Nero said.

Allison and Morgan ran for the front door. Just as Morgan closed the door behind them, the rain roared across the grass in a solid sheet. When it struck the house, the building shook as if a giant bucket had been emptied against the west wall.

Morgan leaned against the door and grinned. "Close, wasn't it?"

"Poor Nero," Allison said. "He'll think he's drowned."

Madame Fifi hurried into the front room to see if the door and windows were closed. She was grotesquely fat, a huge, shapeless mass of painted, powdered, greedy flesh topped by a curly blonde wig that didn't fit. She never wore a corset and her dress appeared to be testing every seam.

She stopped, surprised to see them.

"Well, well," she said. "The pride of Company A. I suppose you're here for business and not to get out of the storm."

"Certainly," Allison said. "We know you have principles."

"You're damned right I do," she snarled. "The girls are eating supper so you'll have to wait."

"We can't stay that long," Allison said. "We'll just have a beer and go on to camp. We were coming back from the fort, you see, and we saw your welcome light, a beacon for weary travelers. . . ."

"A beer for a roof over your heads during a storm? That's a hell of a good bargain, ain't it?"

"We think so," Allison said smugly.

"I oughta throw both of you back in the rain," she grumbled. "All right, I'll send Chris in."

She turned and waddled back to the kitchen.

"Someday she's gonna get sore at the way you talk to her," Morgan said, "and then we won't get to look at Christine no more."

"Don't worry about her bark," Allison said. "It's a lot worse than her bite. Besides, even a nickel's worth of business is not something she could overlook."

The room had a rough pine bar on one side with a number of shelves behind it filled with bottles. Three poker tables and chairs took up most of the space, but very little poker was played here. The tables were used for drinking and visiting with the girls. A piano stood in one corner. Occasionally the tables and chairs were stacked to make room for dancing, but Fifi discouraged it.

Dancing wasn't part of the business—not the profitable part anyway.

Allison had tried to tell her she could make the dancing pay very well if the customers had to buy drinks for the girls after each dance, but she shook her head stubbornly and said nobody came here just to drink. Allison had quit trying to tell her anything. Nobody could, he thought, and that included Christine.

Allison and Morgan sat down at a table near the door and listened to the rain pound against the house. Morgan shook his head. "It's gonna be hell driving to camp in this, Dave. You reckon Fifi would let us stay the night?"

"She'd let us drown first," Allison said. "Forget it."

Christine came in, smiling as she crossed the room. She was a small girl, scarcely five feet tall, with honey blonde hair and eyes that were more violet than blue. She brushed her hair back from her forehead and tied it with a red ribbon, letting it fall down her back almost to the waist. Christine's figure was as nearly perfect as Nature would allow. She always dressed attractively, and tonight her black dress with the gold trim at the neck and sleeves did wonders for her.

Once Christine had confided to Allison that she made all her own dresses. He was not as naïve as Morgan, who believed everything the girl told him, but he did believe what she said about her clothes. Morgan believed Christine was as virtuous as an angel. Allison wasn't so sure, but as he watched her come to their table, he had to admit that her air of demure innocence was astonishing for a girl raised in a place like this.

"Good evening, gentlemen," she said. "What will you have?"

"Beer," Allison said. "We can't stay long."

"You'll want to stay till the storm's over," she said, "so make the beer last."

She brought the beer to them, then sat down at the table, her right hand sliding under the green top to search for and hold Allison's hand. This was strictly against the rules. Fifi had laid down the law when she opened the place. Christine must not show the slightest affection for any customer, but she disobeyed the rule whenever she was with Allison.

Morgan leaned forward, his eyes shining. "You sure are pretty tonight, Christine."

"Thank you, Johnny," she said, glancing briefly at Allison. "It's a new dress."

"I thought it was," Allison said. "I hadn't seen it before."

"Do you like it?"

"Sure I do."

She sighed. "I always have to pump you, and your opinion is the only one that matters."

Allison wondered if she talked that way to other men. He didn't think so. At least he hadn't heard any of them bragging, and they would, he thought, if they had any encouragement from her. She was always cool and distant with the others, and with Allison, too, when there was a crowd.

He didn't pretend to understand her, but it had been this way between them from the first time they had met. If it had not been for his bitter memories, he could have fallen in love with Christine. He instinctively liked her, but love was something else.

"Better start drinking your beer," she whispered. "Fifi's coming."

Allison ignored his beer and grinned as Fifi tromped across the room, the floor squeaking under her weight. Before she reached their table, he said: "We had a little affair with some Indians this morning, Fifi. You'd better keep a look-out for a while."

"Indians?" She snorted contemptuously. "You're a liar, Allison. All you want to do is keep my mind off your slipping in here to get out of the rain. Well, sir, it's almost stopped, so finish and git."

Allison leaned back in his chair. He said blandly: "I keep wondering about your name, Fifi. I'll bet it was Lizzie Glutz. Your real name, I mean."

"My name is Fifi Laffite, damn it."

Allison laughed. "That's the first time I ever heard you claim Laffite for your last name, but it might be right. If I remember my history correctly, Jean Laffite was a pirate. I'll bet you descended from a long line of pirates."

Her big hands fisted. "I oughta hit you right in the snoot. My pa wasn't no pirate."

"Where were you born?" Allison asked. "Kalamazoo? Oshkosh? Paducah?"

"Aw, go to hell," she snarled, and lumbered back into the kitchen.

"I don't know how you do it, Dave," Christine said. "Nobody else can talk to her the way you do."

"I told him a while ago he oughta quit it," Morgan said, "or she won't let us come in here no more."

"Oh, she won't keep you from coming in," Christine said. "She never does anything to stop business." She glanced quickly at the kitchen door. "The rain stopped, hasn't it?"

"I guess it has, Chris."

She leaned toward him. "Dave, I want to talk to you outside. Go out and wait along the west side of the house. It's dark there. I'll join you in a minute. Johnny, if Fifi comes in and asks about us, tell her Dave went to get the horses and I had to go out back."

Morgan nodded. "Sure, I'll tell her."

Allison hesitated, not sure what Christine had in mind, and worried about Morgan. The boy was in love with Christine, but he asked nothing of her.

Even harder to understand was his good-natured attitude. He never seemed upset over her obvious affection for Allison.

"Fifi will raise Cain if she figures out what happened," Allison said.

"She won't," Christine said. "Hurry."

He rose, laid a coin on the table, and went outside. The rain had stopped, but the wind was still cold and damp. He slipped around the corner and waited. Christine came in less than a minute. She put her hands on his shoulders and stood very close to him, breathing hard. Then she said: "Dave, I shouldn't have done this. It isn't right for you to have dreams about me."

He sensed a desperate tone in her voice, as if she had to reach out to someone and there was no one else. She raised her hands to the back of his head and pulled it down. He kissed her then, and in that instant everything changed. Christine's lips burned away the hurt that Fran had left in him.

She drew back, whispering: "Dave, Dave, I've wanted that for so long. I'm a good girl, Dave. You've got to believe me. You've got to."

"I do," he said. "I want to. I want to dream about you, too."

"Dave, listen to me now. I'll be eighteen in two or three months. Fifi says I've got to go to work then. Not with the riff-raff that comes in here. She's been saving me for someone big. An officer, maybe, who will set me up in a house in

Cheyenne. Or maybe a rich cattleman or banker. Anyone who's got money. I don't know how she means to work it and I don't care. All I know is I just can't do it. I won't. I'll run away. I'll kill myself if that's all I can do."

"She's not your aunt, is she?"

"She is, though," Christine said bitterly. "My mother died when I was born. She was beautiful and Fifi knew I would be, too. That's why she raised me. The only reason. She says I'll make her rich."

"I'll get you out of here," he said. "I don't know how, but I will."

She kissed him, a short kiss that was little more than the touch of her lips against his. Then she said: "Please, Dave. I'll do anything you want, go anywhere you want, if you'll get me out of here."

"I will," he promised. "Send Johnny out to the barn. It's time we got started."

"I'll tell him," she said, and disappeared.

He stood there for a time, thinking. His pay never lasted through the month. He was sure Christine had no money, either. And he didn't know where he could borrow a dime.

He walked around the house to the barn and found another soldier with Nero. Reaching the cone of light falling from the lantern that hung from a rafter, he saw that it was Hank Abel of Company K.

Abel said: "I was all set to go in, Allison. Don't

get the notion I was afraid of you and that tub of lard you came with."

Abel played much the same role in Company K that Pete Risdon played in Company A, and the rivalry between the two outfits went back a long time. Many matches had taken place between them, sometimes single fights back of the stables, sometimes team affairs with three or four picked men from each company. Now, in the murky light falling from the lantern, Allison wondered if Abel's presence here was sheer accident, or if it meant something.

"No, I didn't have the notion you were afraid," Allison said finally. "If you're looking for a fight, I'll oblige here and now."

"Not now." Abel's meaty lips drew back from his scraggly teeth. "But, you know, it's kind of funny about the Company A boys back at the fort. They're all yellow. They keep telling us their best fighting men are out at the hay camp, but that's a damned lie, ain't it?"

"I don't know," Allison answered. "It strikes me things must be pretty dull around the fort."

"Sure is, except for the talk about a big campaign against Sitting Bull," Abel said. "A man's got to find some excitement. Or make it if he can't find it."

"Maybe that's why you're here," Allison said.

"You might say that," Abel said. "I came to leave a message, but as long as you're here I'll give it to you personally. Four of us from Company K will be here Saturday night. We want the place to ourselves. We want all the girls and all the whiskey and all the dancing. If any sons-of-bitches from Company A show up, why, by God, we'll throw 'em out."

Allison sensed that Johnny Morgan was standing behind him. He made a half turn so he could still watch Abel. He said: "What does that sound like, Johnny?"

"Like a challenge," Morgan said. "I guess we'd better be here."

Abel guffawed and slapped his leg. "Naw. We won't see hide nor hair of a Company A man Saturday night. Yellow! That's what they are."

"I'll tell Pete Risdon," Allison said.

"I don't want Pete," Abel said. "I want you, if you show up, my fine-feathered cock. I'll pull every feather you've got."

He strode past them to the house. Allison said: "Let's roll, Johnny."

Morgan didn't say anything until they were on the road and headed for the hay camp, wheels and hoofs sloshing in the mud. Then he asked: "Who'll the four be, Dave?"

"Risdon, Jones, and me are three," Allison said. "I don't know about the fourth."

"Me," Morgan said. "I know I was too scared this morning to shoot at the Indians. I sure ain't no fighter. But I want to try."

"We'll see, Johnny," Allison said, and thought bleakly that if Morgan actually had his way, it would be three against four—the toughest four men in Company K.

CHAPTER ELEVEN

At breakfast, Allison told the rest of the detail about Hank Abel's challenge. Pete Risdon's eyes glowed. He turned quickly to Jones.

"What about it, Corporal?"

Jones sighed. "Seems to me there's plenty of fighting men at the fort, but I guess we're the ones they want to whup." He nodded to Allison. "Like Abel saying he'd take you."

"Well, who goes?" Risdon asked. "I can tell you right now I'm gonna be sore if you don't take me."

"You're automatically included," Jones said. "Me, I'm too old and I've been through too many." He rubbed a cauliflower ear and grinned wryly. "But I guess I'll have to go."

"And Dave?" Risdon pressed.

Jones said: "How about it, Dave? You're young and ornery enough to enjoy it."

"I won't enjoy it," Allison said, "but I'll go. Funny, though. We're here to fight Indians, but instead of that we fight among ourselves."

"Human nature," Jones said. "I've never seen a bunch of soldiers who didn't fight among themselves if they weren't fighting somebody else. Company K would forget all about us if the Indians showed up."

"They won't," Risdon said. "I hope Abel brings Clay Moore with him. He's my meat if he does. I whipped him once and he claims I can't do it again." He rubbed his chin, then added: "We're still short a man."

"I know," Jones said, his gaze raking the others. "If one of you don't volunteer to fight for Company A, I'll appoint a man."

"I'll go," Morgan said.

"You?" Risdon said contemptuously. "Hell, kid, you couldn't fight your way out of a room filled with solid air."

"I won't learn any younger," Morgan said. "I figure I've got to try."

"He deserves a chance," Allison said.

"Then you'll be fighting two men," Risdon said. "If I've got Moore, he'll be all I can handle."

"All right, I'll fight two men." Allison shrugged. "Johnny knows he's got something to make up for. If I wind up fighting two men, I'll never open my mouth again about giving him another chance."

"You won't need to," Morgan said. "I won't deserve another chance and I won't ask for it."

"We'll do the best we can," Jones said wearily, "and it had better be good or we'll wind up in the hospital."

Allison had not read his father's letter. He walked out into the April sunshine, thinking that he should have read it last night. But he knew exactly what the letter would say and he had put it off as he did any unpleasant task.

He squatted beside the shed and tore the envelope open. Then a shadow fell across the ground. He glanced up and saw Pete Risdon looking down at him.

"I'm cleaning out the stable and I seen you over here," Risdon said. "Thought I'd come over and gab a while."

"I've got a letter from my father," Allison said. "I haven't read it yet."

"Well, why the hell don't you?" Risdon asked amiably.

Allison didn't answer for a moment. Risdon had never made friendly overtures before. Ever since Risdon had joined Company A he had known he'd have to fight the man sooner or later for no better reason than to find out who could whip the other. Now here was Risdon squatting beside him, his ugly face as pleasant as Allison had ever seen it.

"I figured he'd write something I wouldn't want to read," Allison said finally.

"Why would your pa write something you wouldn't want to read?" Risdon said. "Don't make no sense."

"Nothing does, I guess," Allison said. "He's a preacher, Pete. He's honest about what he believes and what he preaches. He just doesn't understand. That's the trouble. He'd think I was sure going to hell if he knew I'd stopped at the hog ranch last night and talked to Christine."

"Don't tell him," Risdon advised. "What he don't know won't hurt him. He'll never find out how wicked you are."

"He'll want me to come home," Allison said. "Stay with him. Go to his church. Help him with the farm work. I'm all he's got. I can't do it, Pete. I could have at one time, before I knew that there was another world Pa doesn't know anything about. Now I couldn't even take a wife home."

"A wife?" Risdon looked at him as if he had gone completely crazy. "You don't have no wife and I sure don't know where you're gonna get one right away." Then his face took on the tight, mean expression that Allison had seen too many times. "Don't never take a wife, boy. Women like the ones at the hog ranch are all right, all of 'em except that damned uppity Christine. Get 'em into bed and knock hell out of 'em. That's what God made 'em for."

Risdon stood up, his hands fisting and opening and fisting again. Then he burst out: "They oughta be killed. All of 'em except the ones we use for brood mares. What they want a man for is to have somebody handy they can hurt. They ought to be hurt like they hurt us."

Risdon wheeled and strode away. Watching him, Allison remembered what Walt Staley had said— that some woman had hurt Risdon and made him hate all women. Well, Allison told himself, he had been hurt, too, but that didn't make him hate all women. He opened his father's letter and began to read.

Dear Son:

I have not heard from you for a long time and I am concerned about you. The newspapers are full of talk about an extensive campaign against the Sioux this summer. Apparently General Crook will lead one of the main columns against the Indians, so you will probably be in a battle before your enlistment is up. I pray that you will be kept safe and well, and that God will bring you back to me as soon as you are out of the Army.

I have built another room to the house so you will have one of your own. I'm sure you will be married someday even though you think now you will not. I talked to the judge about your reading law again in his office, and he said he would be glad to take you back. He says you probably have matured in the years you have been away.

I haven't told you this before, but it's time that I did. Ever since you left, I have been saving money for you to use when you come home. I have more than $100. I have little need for money, so I will give it to you as soon as you get here.

The weather has been fine lately, although spring is late. We have had so much rain that the ground is too wet to plow, but I think I will be able to start soon.

Please write and tell me about yourself. People ask me about you every Sunday, but I am ashamed to admit that I don't know where you are or what you are doing.

With all my love,

Your father

Allison slipped the paper back into the envelope and shoved it into his pocket. He would write tonight.

"Hey, Dave!" Morgan called. "The corporal says we've got to take another load of hay to the fort."

Allison rose and walked toward the corral. He'd have a talk with Christine. She didn't know much about him and he'd better know a lot more about her than he did. If they went back to Illinois, could they think up a lie about her family that his father would believe? One thing he knew. If they tried to live in his father's world, they would have to live by his rules.

CHAPTER TWELVE

Allison drove the wagon Saturday night, Corporal Jones beside him on the seat. Risdon and Morgan sprawled out in the wagon bed behind them. The sky was clear, the stars and half moon giving enough light to hold the horses at a good pace until Allison turned off the road and pulled into the front yard of the hog ranch.

Nero appeared out of the shadows around the adobe corral and took the team. Allison said: "Company K boys here yet?"

"No, suh," Nero answered. "They ain't showed up."

"They're yellow," Risdon said.

"They'll show," Jones said sharply.

They went into the house. It was near midnight. Madame Fifi was behind the bar, the kitchen door was closed, and none of the girls was in sight. Fifi stared sourly at the four soldiers.

"You boys are late," she said. "The girls are in bed, but I'll get 'em up if you tell me who you want."

"No," Jones said. "Just a beer apiece."

She snorted as she set the beers on the bar. "You're the last of the big spenders, ain't you, Corporal?"

"The very last one, Fifi."

"Where's Christine?" Allison asked.

"You'd like to see her, huh? Well, you ain't going to. She's in bed getting her beauty sleep like any girl her age ought to be. Now forget her. She ain't for the likes of you, soldier."

"Oh, ain't she now?" Risdon said. "What the hell do you mean by that?"

"She ain't for no private," Fifi snapped. "She's too good for your kind."

"Saving her for an officer, huh?" Risdon sneered. "I sure ain't seen no officers come out here to this lousy place. What are you fixing to do, show her off at the fort?"

"None of your damned business," Fifi said. "Drink your beer and skedaddle."

"Looks like we'd better find out about Christine." Risdon glanced at Allison. "If you want to see her before our friends show up, I'll get it out of this old bitch."

Allison was surprised, as he had been every time Risdon seemed friendly. There had been several occasions like this since the morning they'd had their brush with the Indians. Allison had no explanation for it, but as he had told Johnny Morgan, there was no sense looking a gift horse in the mouth.

"I'd like to see her, all right," Allison said.

Risdon swung around to face Fifi. "Where is she?"

"I told you she was in bed."

"Then take Dave to her room."

"Who the hell do you think you are?" Fifi screamed. "I wouldn't take the general himself into Christine's room."

Risdon started along the bar, made the turn at the end, and moved slowly behind it toward Fifi.

"Hold it, Pete," Jones said. "We ain't here to fight women."

Risdon stopped and looked at Jones. "Corporal, I ain't sure this thing is a woman. Besides, I ain't fixing to fight her. I'll just beat hell out of her and then I'm gonna take my knife and cut off both ears and her nose. By that time, she'll be damned glad to . . ."

"All right," Fifi said shakily.

For the first time since he had met Fifi, Allison felt compassion for her. At best Pete Risdon was a brutal-appearing man. Now, he seemed more animal than man.

"All right, what?" Risdon demanded.

"She's in the kitchen," Fifi said.

Risdon jerked his head at Allison. "Go see if she's there, Dave. If she ain't, I'll start to work."

Allison strode to the door and opened it. Christine was sitting at the table, a coffee cup in front of her. No one else was in the room.

"She's here, Pete!" Allison called.

"Too bad," Risdon said as he came back around the bar. "I was gonna enjoy that piece of work.

Get your gabbing done, Dave. They'll be here pretty soon if they're gonna be here at all."

Allison sat down at the table and took Christine's hands. They were stone cold, and her face was pale. She whispered: "Can't you call this fight off? There's no reason for it, is there?"

"No reason at all," he said. "That's not what I wanted to talk about. I've been thinking about you ever since I was here the other night, Christine."

She smiled, then leaned forward and kissed Allison. "I'm glad," she whispered. "I've thought of you ever since I saw you the day this place opened. You aren't like the rest of the soldiers, Dave."

"We talked about getting you out of here," Allison said, "but not about what we'd do after you were out. Meanwhile I've got some things to tell you about myself, Christine."

As briefly as he could, he told her his story. He did not mention Franny Knowles, but he put all the other facts of his life before her.

"What you've got to think about is that I don't have more than sixty dollars to my name," he said. "You can't save much when you're only getting thirteen a month. I had a letter from my father, Christine. He wants me to come back and start reading law again. He said he'd saved a hundred dollars that he could give me. But that's not much, and it will be a long time before I can start a law practice and even longer before I can expect to make a living."

She was leaning forward, her face close to his.

"What are you trying to say to me, Dave?"

"I wanted you to know something about me before I asked you to marry me," he said. "We've talked before, but we never really said anything. You see, I don't have much to give you, but I am asking you to marry me, knowing what little I have to offer."

"Honey," she whispered, "I would marry you if you didn't have a penny, but I want you to be sure you want me. You know the kind of mother I've got. You know where you found me. If your father knew . . ."

"He doesn't need to know," Allison said. "I've thought about it. I still want you to marry me."

"I'll be a good wife, Dave. I promise. . . ."

"Dave, get out here!" Risdon called. "They're coming in!"

CHAPTER THIRTEEN

Hank Abel stepped in first. Clay Moore followed. He was taller than Risdon, but not as heavy. The next was a big redhead Allison had never seen before. He was about Johnny Morgan's age, and Allison had a feeling he was much like Morgan, still holding some of his boyhood fat on his big-boned body.

The fourth was a short, blocky man Allison knew only as Stub. He had scars around his eyes and a nose bent to one side. He appeared to be about Jones's age, too old to enjoy fighting, but still called upon because of his experience.

"Take your fight outside!" Fifi screeched. "If you bust up my place, I'll turn you in!"

No one paid any attention to her. The four Company K men began peeling off their shirts. Out of the corner of his mouth Allison said to Johnny Morgan: "Take the redhead."

Morgan nodded, eyeing the man. He looked scared, but so did the young redhead.

Allison peeled off both his shirt and undershirt and started toward Hank Abel. Within a matter of seconds Company A had squared off against Company K. The redhead moved toward Jones, but Morgan reached him first and drove a fist into his soft belly. The redhead wheeled on him and promptly knocked him down.

Morgan crashed into a poker table on his way to the floor and smashed it flat. Allison heard Fifi shriek an oath, and after that he was too busy to keep track of Morgan.

Abel came in fast, both fists swinging, apparently with the idea of ending it immediately. Allison swung aside, making Abel miss. Then he caught the Company K man with a flicking right on the side of the head. Abel's charge carried him past Allison. He swung back and threw a right. Allison tipped his head just enough, then caught Abel's nose with a sledging right that brought a burst of blood and a shout: "Stand still and fight, damn it!"

Allison had no intention of standing still. He wheeled away each time Abel rushed him, taking his opponent's blows on elbows and shoulders, and all the time he kept ripping through Abel's guard with a fast left that the bigger man couldn't block. Within three minutes he had cut Abel's face to ribbons, but Allison knew he wasn't hurting the soldier enough to knock him out. Sooner or later he would be forced to fight Abel's kind of fight.

It came sooner than he expected. Somehow Abel backed him up against the bar and caught him before Allison could slide clear. He got his arms around Allison and squeezed.

"I'll make you damned sorry you ever saw

Christine," he muttered, and then slammed the top of his head against Allison's face.

Stars exploded in front of Allison. He felt blood spurt from his nose and he knew, if he didn't break Abel's bear hug, he was finished. He threw himself sideways and gained just enough space to bring a heel smashing down on Abel's instep.

The man grunted in pain, his grip relaxing. Allison broke free. Blood ran into his mouth. He tasted it, and suddenly he was angry. He had never been a man to fight well until he got mad, and Abel's butting tactics had done the trick.

Abel came in again with one of his bullish rushes, and this time Allison stood his ground. He timed his first blow perfectly, catching Abel on the Adam's apple. Abel toppled forward, his hands dropping to his sides, his mouth springing open. Allison nailed him on the jaw with a hard-swinging right that had all his weight behind it. Abel went down, out cold.

Allison stepped back, breathing hard. Something hit him on the side of his head and he spilled forward across Abel's body. He rolled over on his back and saw the big redhead looming over him, pulling a foot back to kick him in the ribs.

Allison tried to put his hands out to grab the foot, but he couldn't seem to move fast enough. He raised his hands just off the floor and that was as far as he could get them. The redhead intended to smash his ribs and he couldn't stop it.

Johnny Morgan came out of nowhere, one eye closed and blood streaming down his face. He jumped on the redhead's back, his arms closing around the man's back, his legs circling and squeezing his hips. The kick that would have smashed Allison's ribs never landed.

The redhead staggered under Morgan's weight. He tried to reach back and pull Morgan off, but Morgan grabbed a fistful of hair in his left hand, yanked his head back, and began pounding his face with his right fist. Finally, in desperation, the redhead went over backward. Morgan hit the floor hard and lost his grip.

The redhead staggered upright. He drew back his trusty foot, ready to kick Morgan. But now Allison had managed to stand. He wobbled forward. He rammed into the redhead's back, knocking him flat.

Morgan came to his knees. The big K Company boy shook his head of red hair and started to struggle to his feet. Morgan jumped on his back and smashed his head against the floor. A silent bugle blew taps for the redhead.

Allison helped Morgan up, then looked around. Risdon had just finished his job. Clay Moore was sitting on the floor, leaning against the wall, his mouth sagging open, his eyes glassy.

Jones was in trouble with Stub, who had backed him into a corner and was slugging him with one fist and then the other. The corporal's head swung from side to side like a punching bag. Allison didn't know what was holding Jones up. The corporal would be hurt badly if he didn't get help.

Allison said: "Let's throw the bastard out, Johnny."

He and Morgan came up behind Stub, and caught his arms and lifted him off the floor.

"Wait till I get his feet!" Risdon yelled.

Stub cursed and tried to kick, but Risdon caught both feet. They carried him outside and threw him halfway to the adobe corral.

"You show up in here again and we'll break your god-damn' neck," Risdon said.

They went back in. Jones had staggered to a poker table and sat down, holding his head in both hands. The others dragged the rest of the Company K men outside. Abel was the last. He had come to, but there was no more fight left in him.

"About Christine," Allison said. "I'm telling *you* to stay away from her."

They went back into the house and shut the door. Jones was still at the poker table holding his head. Allison told Fifi to bring him a drink of whiskey.

Christine came out of the kitchen. She caught Allison's arms and held him.

"You aren't hurt, are you, Dave?"

"Just a little here and there," he said, and wondered if Abel had broken any ribs.

She kissed him and held him, her head against his shirt. She started to cry, then regained control of herself. Allison wondered what she had done to interest Hank Abel so much that he had worked up this fight. He didn't ask. He had no need to.

"Abel wanted me, and he was jealous," she said. "I told him I was in love with you, and he said he'd fix it so nobody could love you. I guess I'm to blame for the fight. If I hadn't told him how I felt about you, he wouldn't have come tonight."

Allison didn't know Fifi was there until she stepped in front of him. A fat hand slapped Christine's cheek so hard that the girl staggered halfway back to the kitchen door and almost fell before she regained her balance.

"Git to your room!" Fifi screamed. "I've told you this two-bit private ain't for you."

For the second time that night anger took possession of Dave Allison. He grabbed Fifi and swung her around to face him. He gripped both shoulders and shoved her against the wall. He jammed his right forearm against her windpipe.

Her face turned red, her mouth sprung open, and her brown tongue lolled between her lips so she looked like an idiot. Morgan and Risdon pulled Allison back, and Risdon shook him hard. "Sure, the bitch needs killing, but they'll hang you if you do. She ain't worth it."

The red haze in front of Allison's eyes slowly faded. He moistened his lips, and then he said:

"Fifi, or whatever your god-damned name is, don't ever lay a hand on Christine again. Next time there won't be anybody to pull me off."

Fifi raised a fat hand and massaged her fat throat.

"You busted up my place and you tried to kill me," she croaked. "I'll turn you over to the provost marshal. You'll spend the rest of your life in the guardhouse."

"You do that," Risdon said, "and we'll come back with every man in A Company. We'll take this place down board by board and start you walking toward Cheyenne as naked as the day you was born."

"Get out of here," Fifi whispered hoarsely. "Don't never come back. Any of you."

Allison drove back to the hay camp, Risdon sitting beside him. Jones and Morgan sprawled on their backs on the wagon bed. Jones admitted he hurt everywhere that wasn't too numb to hurt.

"This is my last brawl," Jones said. "I'm too old for it any more."

"After this Johnny can take your place," Risdon said. "You done good, Johnny. How many times did you get off the floor?"

"I dunno," Morgan said. "I lost count."

"Takes a good man to get off the floor as often as you did," Risdon said. "Every time I had a chance to look, you was either hitting the floor or getting up. Except once when I seen you taking a piggy-back ride." Risdon slapped his leg and laughed. "I guess Company K won't be looking for a fight with us again."

They rode on in silence.

Allison thought about Christine. He wondered why he loved her, if there really was a why to a thing like that. He had told her about himself, but he still knew very little about her. Maybe it was better if he never knew much about her.

After Franny Knowles, he had told himself over and over again that he would never, could never, love another woman. But he had been wrong. Christine's beauty had little to do with it. Maybe it was just that a man needed to feel he loved someone and was loved in return.

They would be moving against the Sioux in a few weeks, or even a few days. He might be killed. But he would not die alone and empty.

Allison glanced at Risdon. The man's battered mouth held a smile at the corners. He was living the fight again in memory. If he died in the coming campaign, he would go out, unloving and unloved. It would indeed be a sorry end to a man's life.

CHAPTER FOURTEEN

Patrick O'Hara considered himself the ace of the Chicago *Herald* staff. Humility, he was proud to say, and often did, was not one of his virtues. He stood five feet, six inches tall, he weighed one hundred and twenty pounds after a big meal, and his hair was as red as a fiery sunset. Though three generations removed from County Cork, his Irish blood was as pure as that of his great-grandfather.

He knew and admired George Armstrong Custer, and had followed his trials and tribulations closely with great sympathy. He defended Custer fiercely every time he heard the general attacked, and argued that Grant and the other armchair types who held Custer down to his official rank of lieutenant colonel were jealous of a fighting general who could go out and whip the Indians.

O'Hara read everything he could get his hands on about the forthcoming campaign in which Sitting Bull and his hostiles would be crushed finally and irrevocably. It wasn't that he lacked sympathy for the Indians. He knew as well as anyone that the Sioux had been cheated.

The point was, neither the Indians nor the United States government or the Army or any power on God's earth could hold back the tide of settlement, particularly when gold had been

discovered, and gold had certainly been discovered in the Black Hills. This was the hard,
solid core of the matter, and such niceties as honor
and solemn treaties didn't really change anything.

O'Hara wanted to be out there and see Custer in
action. He wanted it more than anything else in
the world and had even considered resigning and
going to Fort Abraham Lincoln and joining the 7th
Cavalry as a correspondent. But it might not be
that easy. If he didn't have the proper credentials,
they probably wouldn't let him go along. So he
waited, hoping that tough old Samuel Simpson
Cunningham, the *Herald* publisher, would send
him. He waited, and he waited.

He had just about given up hope when
Cunningham called him into his office one
Friday afternoon early in May. Cunningham
leaned back in his swivel chair and scowled as
O'Hara banged into the room and slammed the
door behind him.

"For God's sake, O'Hara," Cunningham said, his
white mustache bristling. "Do you always have to
come in here like a gale off Lake Michigan?"

"Yes, sir," O'Hara said. "I mean, no, sir. I
understand you want to see me."

"I did, but I'm not sure now that you're here."
Cunningham motioned to a chair and tongued his
half-chewed cigar to the other side of his mouth.
"You were in Colorado for a while, weren't you?"

"Yes, sir." O'Hara sat on the edge of his chair

like a bird about to take off. "I worked for the *Rocky Mountain News*."

"You were with the Sir Cedric Smith hunting party, I believe."

"That's correct."

"And after that you joined the staff of the *Cheyenne Leader*?"

A pulse began throbbing in O'Hara's temple. Cunningham knew all this. There wasn't any sense in going over it again, and he needed a little time to pack before he caught the train. But you didn't blow up in Cunningham's face. Not the second time anyhow. So O'Hara said—"Yes, sir."—and held a tight rein on his temper.

"Well, then," Cunningham said, "you know something about Wyoming."

"I sure do," O'Hara said. "I can catch a west-bound train tonight and be in Bismarck sometime Sunday morning."

"Bismarck?" Cunningham said, his mustache bristling again. "Why Bismarck?"

"Fort Abraham Lincoln is close to Bismarck," O'Hara said. "That's where the Seventh Cavalry is stationed. I haven't heard whether General Custer has been returned to his command or not, but I would think they'd have reinstated him before now. They're certainly going to need him in this campaign."

Cunningham acted and looked as if he were about to have apoplexy. The veins stood out on his forehead like blue cords and he rose and slammed his cigar into a spittoon. He pounded the desk with his fist. "My God, O'Hara, I know you claim humility is not one of your virtues, but now you're disowning patience, also. Do you have *any* virtues?"

"Yes, sir," O'Hara said. "I'm a hell of a good reporter."

Cunningham sat down. He held his head until his pulse slowed, and then he said: "The good Lord created you, O'Hara. I admit that. But I'm glad He didn't create twins and give me both of you."

"Yes, sir," O'Hara said. "But if He had, we wouldn't both be working on the *Herald*."

"Why not?"

"Because," O'Hara said simply, "both of us couldn't stand taking orders from you."

In spite of himself, Cunningham laughed. He said: "All right, but since you're not twins, you will take orders from me. I admit you're a good reporter. If you weren't, I wouldn't be sending you to cover this Indian campaign. However, you are not going to Fort Abraham Lincoln."

Cunningham leaned back in his chair and pointed a forefinger at O'Hara. "You are going to Omaha and you will get permission from General George Crook to accompany him. He commands the Department of the Platte with headquarters in Omaha. From there you will go to Cheyenne, then to Fort Laramie. I don't know when the expedition will leave. Perhaps General Crook doesn't, either, but it's my guess it will get under way sometime late in May or early in June."

O'Hara stared at the floor, his hands fisted on his lap. He had never heard of anything as stupid as this. If Cunningham wanted him to see action, Custer was the one he should go with. But . . .

He looked up. "All right," he said. "I'll see if there's a train out of Chicago tonight."

Cunningham nodded. "Go to the business office and draw your expense money. I suggest that you contact General Sheridan in the morning and ask him to write you a letter of introduction to General Crook. It will not be necessary for you to leave Chicago tonight."

O'Hara rose. He took a long breath and said: "I'll see Sheridan in the morning."

"In case you are underestimating General Crook," Cunningham said, "let me remind you that he made an excellent record in his recent Arizona campaign. Furthermore, General Sherman has publicly stated that Crook is the best Indian fighter in the Army."

Hot words rushed to O'Hara's lips. "Yes, sir," he said. He wheeled and walked to the door.

"Oh, one more thing, O'Hara. If I remember right, you knew that wife murderer, Rice Peters."

"Sure, I knew him," O'Hara said, "but it was never proved that he murdered his wife. He was a bouncer in a saloon and a tough one, all right, but . . ."

"Regardless of that, he's wanted by the police. There is a rumor he joined the Army after he ducked out of Chicago. You may run into him. If you do, we want a story."

"You'll get one," O'Hara said, "if he doesn't murder me on sight."

CHAPTER FIFTEEN

O'Hara left Chicago on the morning of May 6th. The rain drummed a constant tattoo on the window of his coach. He could not help registering the fact that he would have a miserable time riding and camping and trying to write up his experiences in a storm like this. But Patrick O'Hara was never one to dwell on matters unpleasant. A moment later he told himself the sun would be shining by the time he reached Cheyenne and Fort D.A. Russell.

He had bought clothes and a Colt .45 before he boarded the train. In his coat pocket he carried a letter of introduction from General Sheridan. Just one thing bothered him. Crook would probably camp all summer somewhere north of Fort Fetterman while Custer was whipping hell out of Sitting Bull and his Sioux. It was O'Hara luck to have a totally unreasonable boss like Samuel Simpson Cunningham. Who else would order him to report to George Crook instead of George Custer?

But O'Hara luck never stayed bad. Not for long, anyhow. So he settled back in his seat to enjoy the ride and puff on his cigar.

When he reached Omaha, O'Hara took a hack to

Crook's headquarters, and, even though it was Sunday, he found the general at his desk studying reports from Sioux country.

O'Hara had been so impressed by the daring and picturesque personality of George Custer that he was prepared to dislike Crook, or at least to resist him. Instead, the instant he shook hands, he gained an impression of cool, calm strength, and innate dignity that commanded respect.

Crook motioned O'Hara to a chair, and O'Hara watched him as he scanned Sheridan's letter. The general was not in uniform, a fact that did not detract from his personality. He had close-cropped hair, a heavy mustache, and an unusual beard that seemed to part naturally below the point of his chin.

The general finished the letter, leaned back in his chair, and studied O'Hara. *Funny,* O'Hara thought. *If I met him on the street in civilian clothes, I'd still recognize him as a soldier.*

Perhaps it was the steady blue-gray eyes. Or possibly the rugged leanness of the man. He gave the impression that he could start out with his infantry at dawn and march them off their feet before sundown.

"Well, now," Crook said finally, "I don't want you to get the notion that we're headed for a Sunday school picnic. I'm not one to condemn the Sioux for fighting. In fact, I admire Crazy Horse and his braves. They're worthy opponents for any army. Our job is to whip them and make them go back to their reservation. I do not expect it to be an easy campaign."

"I'm not looking for an easy campaign," O'Hara said, "and I'm not altogether a city man. I'm out of practice, but I've done some riding and camping and shooting." He laughed. "I'll admit I never hit the bull's eye."

"It's not that I'm against reporters," Crook said. "I know they have to write what they see and hear. But some of them tend to be critical and to second-guess the commander. I've also met some who groused about the rations and dust and the heat and anything else that came up. The country north of Cheyenne is not a Garden of Eden, so you'll suffer."

"I know what some of it is like," O'Hara said. "I was with the *Cheyenne Leader* for a while, but I never got as far north as Fort Laramie."

Crook reached for a sheet of paper, then picked up a pen and dipped it into the bottle of ink. He wrote for a time and signed his name at the bottom of the sheet.

"When you reach Fort D.A. Russell, give this to Colonel W.B. Royall. I suggest that you buy a good horse and saddle when you get to Cheyenne." He folded the paper and handed it to O'Hara. "As of now, I can't tell you exactly when you will leave Fort Russell, or even when I'll return to Fort Laramie, so you will likely have a few boring days on your hands. I can assure you there won't be many of them."

Crook rose and extended his hand. O'Hara shook it, and asked: "Have you ever heard of a plainsman named Walt Staley?"

"Staley?" Crook smiled. "I've already hired him as a messenger. He's a good man, one of the best on the frontier. You know him?"

O'Hara nodded. "We were both with the Sir Cedric Smith hunting party in Colorado. I've often wondered what happened to him after that."

"You'll meet him again," Crook said. "He'll be with the command at least part of the time."

O'Hara took the cab back to the depot and caught the next train for Cheyenne.

CHAPTER SIXTEEN

When O'Hara stepped off the coach at Cheyenne on Monday, he had the impression that the town had doubled or tripled in size since he had left. He had never seen such a crowd at the depot or so many men milling around the tracks.

Soldiers, miners, cowboys, trappers, freighters, laborers—all bellowing at each other or standing and talking or backing and filling their freight wagons to get a choice position. He saw a couple of Concord coaches waiting beyond the main part of the crowd, and then the truth struck him. The town hadn't actually grown. It just had more business, partly from the military preparing for the coming campaign, and partly from the gold rush to the Black Hills.

For a time he stood motionless on the cinders, watching the flow of the crowd and hearing sounds peculiar to a frontier city. Then a big hand slammed him on the back, driving him forward two steps and knocking the wind out of him.

He labored for a moment to suck air back into his tortured lungs, and then he turned, his fists doubled. He found himself looking up into the grinning face of a big man in buckskin.

"How are you, you little sawed-off, freckled-faced, red-headed Irish bastard?"

"I'm fine," O'Hara said. "And how are you, you wigwam-weaned, buffalo-headed, squaw-loving son-of-a-bitch?"

They shook hands and pounded each other on the back. "How'd you ever find me?" O'Hara asked. "You're too dumb to figure out that I might be climbing off a train to cover the campaign for my newspaper."

"Way too dumb," Walt Staley agreed affably. He picked up O'Hara's bag. "Come on, let's find you a hotel room. Then I'll buy you a drink."

"I've got to get out to the fort," O'Hara said. "I saw General Crook in Omaha and he gave me a letter of introduction. . . ."

"No hurry," Staley was jamming his way through the crowd, O'Hara running to keep up with him. "You've got ten days, maybe more, before any-thing happens. You're gonna grow calluses on your butt, O'Hara."

"I thought we'd be heading out for Fort Laramie in a day or two."

"Naw." Staley shook his head. "It ain't likely. One wing will go from here, but the supplies ain't showed up yet. Not all of 'em, anyway. The other wing moves up from Medicine Bow, which is west of here a piece on the U.P. They'll join up at Fort Fetterman, but neither one's ready yet."

O'Hara sighed as he trotted along beside Staley. Walt knew what he was talking about, but even so, he ought to go to the fort immediately and report to Colonel Royall. He heard the pistol-sharp crack of a whip and a moment later one of the big stagecoaches rolled past him on the street, dust lifting around it, clouding its passage. The coach was crowded to capacity, both inside and out. "Damned Black Hillers," Staley said. "They're the cause of all this trouble. Chances are they'll git their hair lifted before they ever see Deadwood. Lot of Sioux and Cheyennes just riding around between here and there, looking for scalps."

"Then why doesn't the Army clean them out?" O'Hara asked.

Staley shrugged. "You'll have to ask General Crook. I'll admit it takes time to get this big an outfit together. Supplies are coming in every day and they're being hauled to Fort Laramie and then to Fetterman, but, like I said, it takes time. Why it takes so *much* time I don't know."

Staley grinned, a sudden flash of white across his dark face. "Besides, a few stagecoaches getting stopped and everybody murdered might slow this gold rush down a little. I ain't heard that the Army ever invited anybody into the Black Hills."

That was true, O'Hara knew. Legally the miners had no right to be in the Black Hills, so who could honestly blame the Indians if they did lift a few scalps?

O'Hara did not fully appreciate the unpopularity of such thinking until he had taken a hotel room and then gone into the bar for the drink with Staley. The crowd there included all of the types he had seen at the depot, plus a number of neatly dressed gamblers and con men who were trying to get their hooks into the greenhorn Easterners.

Staley elbowed O'Hara. "Watch this," he whispered out of the corner of his mouth. Then he cleared his throat and said loudly: "I never have understood why the good Lord put so many damned fools on earth. There's plenty of 'em right here in this room, thinking they're gonna find gold in the Black Hills."

The conversation around Staley died. The bartender leaned forward anxiously.

"Better not talk that way in here, mister. It ain't wise."

"I'll bet it ain't!" Staley bellowed. "Your Cheyenne storekeepers and freighters and bankers are making a lot of *dinero* out of this Black Hills gold grab. Well, sir, I never was a man to win popularity contests, but I know fools when I see 'em. Any man's a fool who takes out for the Black Hills right now with the country full of Indians. They'll git their hair lifted as sure as hell's hot."

"He's a squawman," someone said in disgust, "trying to scare folks away from the Black Hills."

And another: "Yeah, probably paid by the Sioux to come in here and talk like that. Let's throw him out."

A slender man in a black broadcloth suit with

113

a gold chain across his chest shouldered his way through the crowd. He said: "Get out of here, mister. We don't aim to listen to none of your kind of talk around here."

"A mite touchy, ain't you, Slick?" Staley asked. "You know something about Indians, seems to me. Up there on Wind River they tell me there's a Shoshone girl who's looking for you to come . . ."

The slender man's face turned pale. He went for his gun. Before it cleared leather, Staley had his knife tip pressed against the man's throat. "Go ahead," Staley said. "Give the undertaker a little business."

The man's hand dropped away from the butt of his gun. He muttered: "Get out of here, Staley. Just get out. The drinks are on the house."

Staley reached out with his left hand and lifted the man's gun from the holster. He slipped his knife back into its scabbard, ejected the shells from the revolver, and handed it back. "Thanks for the free whiskey." Staley jerked his head toward the street door. "Come on, Pat."

Outside, O'Hara mopped his sweating face.

"That was a fool trick, wasn't it, Walt? He must have had some tough hands all set to gang up on you."

"Sure he did, but mostly he just wanted me out of there. Someday I'll kill the bastard. He married a Shoshone girl several years ago. She had two of his babies. Then he fell into some money and bought this hotel and kicked her out. She's with her tribe, waiting for him to come back to her. He never will unless he's starving to death."

O'Hara stuffed his wet handkerchief back into his pocket and smiled at Walt Staley. He liked this big, rangy, tough galoot. Walt Staley had a sense of honor that was not shared by the average plainsman.

Knowing this, he was still shocked when Staley told him he wanted to marry a half-breed girl named Tally Barrone.

"I never thought much about her till this spring," Staley said. "She'd always seemed like a little girl who'd had to take over the housework when her ma died. But now she's a woman. I'm going to get her away from her pa and her brothers as soon as I work a month for the Army. Maybe you'll see her before you go back to Chicago. She's one hell of a fine girl."

"If she's your girl," O'Hara said, "she's got to be."

Chapter Seventeen

Staley had to leave Cheyenne the following morning with dispatches for Fort Laramie, but before he rode away, he took O'Hara to a livery stable that was owned by a man he knew and helped him buy a horse. O'Hara admitted that if he had been left to his own devices, he would have ended up with an old nag that wouldn't have carried him as far north as Lodgepole Creek.

They were lucky to find a flat-shouldered, gentle, reasonably young brown gelding. Staley pointed out that the animal was the kind the Army liked. "You'll be able to sell him to 'em when you're done with him," Staley said. "You might make a little money on him. At least you won't lose much."

They bought a second-hand saddle and O'Hara rode several blocks and returned to the livery stable. "You'll make out all right," Staley said. "Now I got to get to humping. I'll probably see you at Fort Laramie."

He started to mount his buckskin, then put his foot back on the ground, and turned to O'Hara. "It ain't often I cotton to a man when I first meet him, but I ran into a soldier at a hay camp afore I got to Fort Laramie that I sure like. His name's Dave Allison. He's smart. I keep wondering why he's only a buck private."

"You can be sure there's a good story back of him," O'Hara said, "or he wouldn't be in the Army at all. Maybe I'll meet him after we get started."

"A man like Allison ought to be an officer," Staley said, "but they've got him hauling hay and taking orders from a bone-headed corporal."

"Sometimes there's a reason," O'Hara said. "Maybe this Allison drinks too much. Or fights discipline and spends most of his time in the guardhouse."

"He didn't strike me as being that kind."

"You just reminded me of something," O'Hara said. "I'm supposed to keep my eyes open for a man named Rice Peters. Ever hear of him?"

"Don't think so. Well, I've got to ride."

O'Hara stood in front of the livery stable, watching Staley ride down the crowded street. Finally, Staley disappeared in the heavy traffic, and for some reason O'Hara felt alone in a strange world.

When O'Hara reported to Colonel Royall at Fort D.A. Russell, he was told he would mess with the officers of Company E, 3rd Cavalry. He found a number of reporters at the fort who intended to accompany the Big Horn and Yellowstone Expedition. They represented newspapers in New York, Philadelphia, San Francisco, Omaha, Denver, Cheyenne, and Chicago. It would, O'Hara thought, be the best-reported campaign in the history of Indian warfare.

O'Hara did not leave Fort D.A. Russell with Company E until May 19th, although a larger force had left two days earlier. Crook had been right about the hardships. O'Hara had not ridden a horse for several years, and when the company bivouacked that afternoon, he was so stiff he could hardly move.

Another source of discomfort was the alkaline dust, stirred by the horses' hoofs until the air all along the column seemed to be one great, gray cloud, making breathing almost impossible.

O'Hara drained his canteen and thought he would go out of his mind from thirst. Captain Hanson suggested that he keep a small stone in his mouth. He did, and found that it helped.

By the end of the second day he was not only stiff and thirsty, but hungry and tired as well. He spread his horse blanket on the ground and fell asleep, completely worn out. Later, when someone poked him in the ribs and told him supper was being served in Captain Hanson's tent, he had trouble remembering where he was and why he was here. When he did remember and struggled to his feet, every muscle in his body cried out.

Time was the answer, Captain Hanson told him. In time he would learn that the less water he drank, the better he could march. He would learn to make the water in his canteen last. In time the soreness would work out of his muscles. Why, in time, he said, he might even enjoy riding with the cavalry!

Meanwhile O'Hara appreciated the halts that were made, to let the horses graze and to give the recruits a chance to rest. He was the greenest, softest recruit in the column.

Lashed by rain and slowed by mud, the troops did not reach Fort Laramie until one o'clock on May 24th. They made camp on the prairie, and O'Hara, who had chafed at delay back at Fort D.A. Russell, had never been more thankful in his life.

Captain Hanson sat beside O'Hara in front of his tent and smoked a cigar. Hanson told him the fort was the oldest in the region, having been opened forty years or more ago as a trading post. Some had called it Fort William, others Fort John, but to most it had been Fort Laramie from the start. Here were the crossroads, Hanson said, with an Indian trail running north and south, and the Oregon Trail coming in from Nebraska and going on to South Pass.

Mountain men and emigrants and 'Forty-Niners had all gone this way. Here they found grass and cottonwoods and good water with the Laramie and the North Platte coming together below the fort. Beyond, to the west, Laramie Peak tipped up above the horizon, a symbol of the main chain of the Rockies that lay still farther west.

Now the Army had the fort. Tomorrow the

company would cross the North Platte on a bridge that had been completed only a few months before and head on toward Fort Fetterman, which would be the real jumping-off place for the expedition. As far as this day was concerned, O'Hara told Hanson, he was perfectly happy to do as little as he could.

Walt Staley came out late in the afternoon. He had just returned to Fort Laramie with dispatches from Fort Fetterman. Crook was at Fetterman, and Staley guessed the entire command would be on the move in a few days.

"But, by God, I don't savvy why we ain't moved already," Staley said. "Eighty lodges have pulled out of the Red Cloud Agency in the last few days. They ain't on no picnic. You can count on that. From what I hear, the Indians are thicker'n fleas on a dog between here and the Chug. You didn't run into any on the way up?"

O'Hara shook his head. "The only enemy was rain and mud."

"Well, they were all around you," Staley said. "They've been running off government stock. They killed a Red Cloud mail carrier. A lot of miners on their way back to Cheyenne have lost stock. It's a hell of a situation."

O'Hara studied the scout's dark face. Normally a pleasant man, good-natured and hard to ruffle, today he was sullen and resentful. O'Hara wondered why. He said carefully: "I don't understand how this is supposed to work, Walt. Crook expects to move north, but you're telling me the Indians are active between here and Cheyenne, and that's south."

"These are little bands," Staley said. "Probably they're young bucks who have left the big party and are out to steal stock and pick up all the cheap scalps they can. Some of 'em are probably Cheyenne Dog soldiers."

"But how will Crook stop these little bands?"

"He can't police this whole corner of Wyoming," Staley admitted. "All he can do is to go after the big bunch that is north of here, far as we know. Chances are, when the young bucks hear what's going on to the north, they'll hightail up there and throw in with Crazy Horse before the big fight starts."

"I thought Sitting Bull was running things," O'Hara said.

"He's the one you reporters write about," Staley said, "but Crazy Horse is the fighter. He's a good one, too. The best they've got."

O'Hara still did not understand Staley's bad humor. He decided to risk a feeler.

"Did you see your girl on your way down from Fetterman?" he asked.

Staley gave him a sharp, probing look, then said: "No, I was afraid to. Louie told me to stay away. I'd just be kicking up dust for nothing. I'm not going to see her until I'm ready to get her out of there. And that may be too late. Her brothers might trade her off to the Cheyennes before that."

He paused, staring westward at the setting sun.

"I don't know how to work it, Pat. I'm damned if I do. Even if I ain't too late when I go after Tally, I may have to kill Louie and his boys to get her. How can you expect a girl to love you when you've killed her pa and her brothers?"

O'Hara had no answer to that question. He had no answers at all today. For the first time he admitted the truth to himself. He wished he was back in Chicago. This country out here was just too damned raw for the likes of O'Hara.

CHAPTER EIGHTEEN

Both wings of the Big Horn and Yellowstone Expedition joined at Fort Fetterman, General George Crook assumed command, and on May 29th the column moved out, traveling north from Fetterman on the Bozeman Trail into the unknown.

Crook had one thousand and two men, forty-seven officers, one hundred wagons, and two hundred and ninety-five pack mules. In the final days of the campaign the mules would be his means of transportation, giving him speed and mobility. The guides were Frank Gruard, Louis Richaud, and Baptiste Pourier. Colonel Royall commanded the cavalry, Colonel Alexander Chambers the infantry.

Dave Allison knew few of these facts. He had not been taken into General Crook's confidence. He would march, he would obey orders, and the day his enlistment expired he would get the hell out of the Army.

Allison marched beside Johnny Morgan. He had stuck with Morgan ever since the hay-camp detail rejoined Company A. Fort Laramie had been stripped, leaving barely enough men to defend and maintain it. But Johnny Morgan was still his bunky, Jones his corporal, Muldoon his sergeant, and a young, green West Pointer named Linn had become his lieutenant, and sooner or later they would all be fighting Indians. The Indians called the infantry "walk-a-heaps," which was exactly what they'd be doing, probably all the way to Montana.

His feet hurt. He said so.

Johnny Morgan suggested that maybe they'd be given horses to ride. Mounted infantry would be right nice, he said. And useful, too.

"You're a dreamer, Johnny," Allison said. "We march. We pick 'em up and we lay 'em down. If you don't like it, you'd better join the cavalry. In this outfit shank's mare is the best mount you'll ever have."

"Aw, they wouldn't let me into their old cavalry," Morgan muttered.

Allison grinned. For once in his life the boy was right. But at least they led the column. The column stretched behind them for four miles. The wagons, each pulled by six mules, followed the infantry. The cavalry was next, fifteen companies spaced at intervals so they would not get mixed up with each other.

Glancing back at the long cloud of dust, Allison thanked God the infantry was up front. He had all he could do to swing along in route step without laboring to breathe in that choking blanket of dust.

Allison had been back at the tail end of the line often enough to know how it was. White powder settled on men and horses. It worked into a man's nose and ears, made a harsh, gritting sound between his teeth, and caused his blood-shot eyes to become raw red wounds. Allison had eaten cavalry dust more times than he liked to remember. He considered the relationship today a case of tardy justice.

Someone behind Allison kept trying to play a French harp, but he was getting little music out of the instrument. Pete Risdon yelled an obscene remark and the harpist obliged by putting his instrument away. But then another man started to sing, and Johnny Morgan told Risdon he didn't see that the situation had improved very much.

"It sure as hell ain't," Risdon agreed. "I never made a campaign that didn't have a few musicians along. Right now I wish a thousand Sioux would come riding hell for leather over them hills. It would put a quick stop to the caterwauling."

"You'll have your wish one of these days," Allison said, "and the minute you see all those bucks wearing nothing but a breechclout and war paint, you'll wish you had the harp to listen to instead of their whooping."

Risdon laughed. "I guess you're right. Just goes to prove a man don't want what he's got no matter what it is."

"Or he don't know when he's well off," Morgan said. "Right now I wish I was sitting in Ma's kitchen, watching her make doughnuts. Many's the time I sat there and wished I was having some big adventure in the Army. I always seen myself a wearing a purty brand-new uniform. So here I am in dirty shirt blues that'll probably drop off of me before we get back to the fort."

"And you dreamed of being a hero," Allison added.

"Oh, sure," Morgan said. "I was always a hero."

The command halted for two hours. Horses and mules were fed and watered, the men ate their noon meal of salt pork, hardtack, and coffee. Morgan made the mistake of mentioning his mother's doughnuts.

"It's bad enough trying to choke this garbage down," Risdon said, glaring at the greasy meat. "But having to hear about your ma's doughnuts . . ." He sighed. "I'll bet they melted in your mouth, didn't they, kid?"

"They sure did," Morgan said. "I used to go down to the cellar and fetch up a crock of cold milk. . . ."

"Eat your dinner and forget it," Allison said. "You won't be seeing your ma or her doughnuts for a long time."

They moved out a few minutes later, blanket rolls and haversacks slung over their shoulders, the tin cups that hung from the haversacks banging and jingling down the line. Parades and ceremonies and dreams of heroism did not fit into this foot-slogging column. Cold milk and doughnuts belonged to the limbo of lost boyhood. Here was the hard reality of sweat and thirst and aching feet. The singer and the French-harp player fell silent at last.

They marched twelve miles before making camp on Sage Creek. After the officer of the day assigned an area to Company A, Pete Risdon and Nelse Luckel took buckets and went to the creek for water. Allison and Morgan gathered wood, while others put up tents for the officers.

Allison was squatting by the fire, drinking a cup of coffee when General Crook and an aide cantered by riding toward the head of the column. Crook's beard was braided and tied. He wore a battered slouch hat, a disreputable-looking hunting rig, and moccasins. Allison had heard that he was the sloppiest dresser since U.S. Grant, but his manner and bearing were very military. It just went to prove, Allison thought wryly, that clothes didn't make the general.

Walt Staley strode along the creek, a small, red-headed man trotting to keep up with him. Apparently Staley was looking for Allison, for he moved directly toward him, calling: "How'd you make out today, Dave?"

"I'm tired," Allison said. "I don't have a horse to ride like some fellow I could name."

Staley laughed and motioned toward the red-head. "I fetched a man along I want you to know. You'll get tireder'n you are now just listening to him. Name's Pat O'Hara."

O'Hara shook hands with Allison, his freckled face split by a wide grin.

Johnny Morgan and Corporal Jones and some of the others were lounging around the fire, drinking coffee. Allison introduced them, but O'Hara seemed to be interested only in Allison himself.

"This overgrown lunkhead was with me on the Sir Cedric Smith hunting party in Colorado," O'Hara said, jerking a thumb at Staley. "He ran into me when my train pulled into Cheyenne, took me into a saloon on the pretext of buying me a drink, then tried to start a brawl so I'd get killed."

"But seeing as it didn't work out," Staley said, "I had to fetch him along. I figured that if he didn't get killed in Cheyenne, the Sioux would take care of it up here. They're always looking for red-haired scalps."

"I'm with the Chicago *Herald*," O'Hara said. "I'm going to make Staley the hero of my next article and tell how he saved the entire Yellowstone and Big Horn Expedition by his great personal bravery."

"Then he can go East and start a show," Allison said sourly. "That's how Bill Cody got his reputation . . . and his fortune."

"I've heard that," O'Hara agreed. He studied Allison closely, then said: "I wanted to talk to you because Walt told me you went with him after some Cheyenne horse thieves early this month. Or maybe it was last month."

"He can tell the story better than I can," Allison

said. "Johnny here was along." He motioned to Morgan, who stared at the ground, his face turning red. "So was Pete Risdon." He glanced inquiringly at the men around the fire. "Where did Pete go?"

"He went back to the creek for more water," Luckel said. "I guess he ain't back yet."

"I was curious about why you were in the infantry," O'Hara said. "Walt told me you rode pretty well. After all, a man on foot can't catch Indians."

"That's true," Allison said mildly.

"Of course it's true," O'Hara said. "The Sioux are the best light cavalry in the world."

Very deliberately Allison pulled his pipe out, filled it, and lighted it with a burning twig from the fire. Then he said: "Did you ever hear of the cavalry catching up with the Indians?"

"I reckon he didn't," Staley said. "That's something you ought to inform your city readers about, Pat. The cavalry always takes a load of stuff along, but the Sioux travel light. They outrun the horse soldiers every time."

"Well," O'Hara said, "if that's true, why is this expedition in the field?"

"That's a real interesting question," Staley said. "One thing the cavalry can do is keep the Indians on the move. Or go out in the winter and burn their villages and kill women and children and destroy their grub so they've got to come in or starve. That's the way the yellowlegs whip the Indians, Pat."

O'Hara frowned at Staley, then glanced at Allison. "Sorry, Mister O'Hara," Allison said, "but that is the standard cavalry procedure. Custer did it on the Washita."

"He was obeying orders," O'Hara said sharply.

Another Custer man, Allison thought, and he considered the difference between Crook, who paid no attention to his appearance, and Custer with the long yellow hair, Custer the vain, Custer the cavalier. But it was as useless to discuss Custer with a Custer worshiper as it was to discuss religion with a preacher or politics with a politician. You just wasted your wind and made the other man angry.

"And another thing about your cavalry," Allison said, "which makes me prefer the infantry. We camp, we cook supper, we smoke a pipe, and go to bed. What's your cavalryman doing all this time? He's on the line, taking care of his horse." He shook his head. "I'm satisfied to be a dog soldier until I get my discharge. On the First of July I'll leave the Army and go home."

O'Hara started to say something, but Staley, apparently sensing a growing irritation, said quickly: "We'd better mosey back to Captain Hanson's tent or he'll eat your supper."

"I guess so," O'Hara said reluctantly. "Looks like we'll be together on this campaign for a long time, Allison. I want you to know that I'm just as interested in privates as I am generals. More privates get killed than generals. We'll talk again. If you have any ideas about this expedition that you want to pass on, let me know."

"You can write about the rations," Allison said. "We'll be lucky if we don't all come down with scurvy before we get back to Fort Fetterman."

"I'll fetch in a deer for you tomorrow," Staley said, and walked off with Pat O'Hara.

Allison stared after the two men, his irritation fading. After all, a reporter did have to write about something. Most of the war correspondents slept in the officers' tents and messed with the officers and seldom mentioned a private unless he was a casualty. Still, Allison had no intention of talking about himself to Pat O'Hara. He didn't want to share the story of his private life with people from Maine to Oregon.

Suddenly he realized that Pete Risdon was squatting beside him.

"We just had visitors, Pete. Staley brought along a reporter. He wanted to talk about that little fight we had with the Indians back at the hay camp."

"The redhead with Staley is a reporter?"

"Yes, his name's O'Hara."

"Where's he from?"

"Chicago. Why?"

"I thought he looked familiar," Risdon said. "But I guess I was wrong."

Allison watched him walk away.

CHAPTER NINETEEN

The command marched twenty miles the second day, camping that night on the South Cheyenne River. Staley made good his promise and brought in a deer. He and Pat O'Hara dined on venison with their hosts, Private David Allison and friends, Company A, 9th Infantry.

O'Hara had recovered from his early stiffness. He rode with Captain Hanson and Company E of the 3rd Cavalry and would have enjoyed it if the weather had not turned cold. Officers and men wore overcoats. O'Hara decided he made quite a picture, all bundled up, with his black derby tipped forward over his forehead, his short-stemmed pipe clamped in his teeth, and his carbine canted across his saddle.

That evening O'Hara heard that a private in Captain Meinhold's Company B, 3rd Cavalry, had accidentally shot himself in the thigh. The news depressed O'Hara. It was such a waste. He wrote about it that night beside the campfire. The man had come so far to fight Indians, but he might not live long enough to see a Sioux brave.

Early the following morning General Crook sent Walt Staley back to Fort Fetterman with dispatches. He took O'Hara's articles along with the news stories of the other correspondents. This day, June 1st, was worse than the previous day. Black clouds hung low, giving the sky an ominous, constantly threatening appearance. Snow or sleet fell through the morning, and the cold held on all afternoon.

In spite of bad weather and mud, the command moved twenty-one miles that day, the road following a spine that lay above a series of ravines. O'Hara saw almost no timber except a few stunted junipers that somehow sucked life out of a forbidding land.

They continued to move in a northwesterly direction until they reached the site of old Fort Reno. Here Crook had expected to meet a large band of Crows, but they were nowhere in sight. The Crows were to serve as scouts and add strength to the command. Crook hesitated to push deeply into a country swarming with hostiles until the Crows joined him, so he sent three scouts to locate them and bring them into camp.

O'Hara had not seen Dave Allison since the venison feast. He wanted to know the man better, so he searched the camp until he found Allison, sitting beside a fire with several other soldiers.

As he approached the group, a big soldier got up and walked away. There was something vaguely familiar about the man, but O'Hara shrugged it off. After all, why should he run into anyone he knew in this camp of more than a thousand men gathered from all parts of the country?

Allison offered O'Hara a cup of coffee. So he squatted beside the fire with the soldiers and drank from the tin cup while Allison and Jones hoorawed him about getting bored with the cavalry. If you wanted excitement, they said, you had to come to the infantry.

O'Hara grinned and said he guessed that was right. And then, finishing the coffee, he said: "Allison, let's look over the ruins of the fort. This is the only place I know where Uncle Sam took a beating. I've always been interested in these forts along the Bozeman Trail. That old chief, Red Cloud, sure did raise hell."

Allison chuckled and stood up.

As they walked away from the fire, O'Hara remembered something.

"Who was the big man who left just as I arrived?"

"Pete Risdon."

O'Hara frowned, repeated the name, and shook his head. "Guess I don't know him. He looked kind of familiar when he walked off, but it must have been my imagination."

"He was the one who went chasing the Indian horse thieves with me and Johnny Morgan and Walt Staley," Allison said.

"I remember you mentioned him," O'Hara said. "He's a tough one, Staley says."

"He's tough with a man he can whip," Allison agreed, "but he looks up to a man who can whip him. He bullied Johnny Morgan until we had a set-to with some soldiers from Company K. Since then he thinks Johnny's all right because Johnny kept getting off the floor and never quit fighting."

"A lot of men are like this fellow Risdon," O'Hara said.

They climbed a hill to the fort's cemetery, which was on a lonely bluff overlooking Powder River. O'Hara stopped and looked around, and a lump formed in his throat.

The Indians had wreaked havoc in this abandoned fort. The headboards had been pulled down, the palings ripped off the fence, and what had been a cenotaph built to honor the slain men was now a pile of broken bricks.

The graves of the soldiers who had died here in the fighting of 1866 and 1867 were covered by boulders, and in this moment O'Hara resolved that everyone who read the Chicago *Herald* would be reminded of these men who had given their lives at this lonely and forgotten outpost.

O'Hara picked up what had been a headboard from a pile where they had been carelessly thrown together. He read aloud: "Number Twelve. Private C. Slagle, Company F. Twenty-Seventh Infantry. Killed May Thirtieth, Eighteen Sixty-Seven." He tossed the board back onto the pile and looked at Allison. "Thus we honor the nation's dead," he said.

Allison was standing motionless, his eyes on the

line of graves. Suddenly he wheeled to face O'Hara. "I may have the same future. You, too, O'Hara. It's not so much that I don't want to die, though as a matter of fact I don't. The thing is, there's something I've got to do before I catch a Sioux bullet."

"What is it?" O'Hara asked. "Maybe I can do it for you if you have bad luck."

"No, I don't think you could," Allison said. "I'm sorry I mentioned it."

Allison walked away. O'Hara sighed. He had come close to breaking through the wall that Dave Allison had built around himself, but not close enough. He caught up with Allison, who had stopped to stare at the place where the fort had stood, the fort that now was a ruin of old chimneys and stones and weathered beams and rusty iron.

"Hard to picture the way it looked ten years ago," O'Hara said.

Allison nodded and said nothing. They started back to camp, neither talking. O'Hara, glancing at Allison's hard-set face, saw that the soldier was not in a mood to talk about anything, least of all about himself.

On the way down the hill to the camp they passed an Indian grave. O'Hara had read about Indian graves, but had never seen one before. It was a buffalo hide tied by thongs, probably leather or buckskin, and held off the ground by cotton-wood poles. O'Hara judged it was about six feet high. The body was gone, although who had taken it or why was a mystery.

O'Hara and Allison poked around among some odds and ends scattered on the ground: two blue blankets, one moccasin, a bright colored shawl, and a few other objects. After they left, O'Hara heard men's voices and glanced back to see several soldiers yanking the cottonwood poles down.

"They're after firewood," Allison said. "I don't think they're going to bother the Indian's ghost."

"No, I guess not." O'Hara walked in silence for a time, thinking about it. Then he said: "The Indians desecrated the graves of our soldiers who died defending the Bozeman Trail. Ten years later our soldiers desecrate the grave of an Indian who died defending his homeland."

"You know what Walt Staley would ask?"

"No. What?"

"He'd want to know which was civilized," Allison said. "Well, which is?"

"Neither," Allison answered curtly. "And that includes most of the women, white and red."

They walked back to camp. At last, O'Hara thought, he had a clue to Allison's problem. It had something to do with women. But then, most men's problems had something to do with women.

When they reached Company A, O'Hara said: "Allison, if I can do anything for you . . ."

"Forget it," Allison said. "If I live, I'll do it myself."

137

"And if you don't?"

"It won't get done," Allison said, and turned away. O'Hara just stood there for a while, thinking.

"The hell with it," he said, and went back to the cavalry.

CHAPTER TWENTY

On the night of June 5th the command bivouacked near the site of old Fort Kearney. That evening O'Hara stopped and talked for a time to Allison, who was not familiar with the details of Carrington's expedition ten years before, or of Red Cloud's victory and the abandoning of the forts that Carrington and his men had built and defended so courageously.

"I've read everything I could find about that campaign," O'Hara said. "It's like I told you when we were looking over the ruins of Fort Reno. It's an old story. They send out half enough men to do a job and starve them to death at that."

"It's funny you don't hear much of Red Cloud any more," Allison said.

"Oh, he's a peaceful old bastard now," O'Hara said. "It's Sitting Bull you hear about. And Crazy Horse, who's a real fighting man." He jerked his head to the north. "Yonder a few miles is where Captain Fetterman and his command were wiped out, a total of eighty-two men. Fetterman was a bull-headed man who wouldn't obey orders, so he made his own fate."

O'Hara filled his pipe and stared at the fire. Then he said: "I've always admired General Custer, but he's had a lot of trouble. You wonder about a man like that. He's daring and dashing and he'll find and whip the Sioux if anybody does, but sometimes I get a feeling he's like Fetterman in one way. He makes his own trouble."

Allison agreed silently. He made his own trouble, too. So did Pete Risdon and Johnny Morgan. So did most people.

The next day the column marched seventeen miles.

The following day, June 7th, the private who had accidentally shot himself was buried. Allison found the funeral even more depressing than most funerals. He heard Captain Henry read the burial service from the *Book of Common Prayer*; he saw a handful of dirt thrown upon the body as the trumpets sounded taps, and the grave was filled and he marched away with his company.

The man had been killed by his own carelessness, Allison supposed, and he was surprised when O'Hara came to visit him, wanting to talk about the incident. There was honor fighting and dying in battle, O'Hara said, but an accident like this was a terrible waste. There was no honor in it.

O'Hara was close to tears as he talked. Allison had never seen him so upset. He suspected that some of O'Hara's superficial cockiness was not really cockiness, and that his digging into other people's business was at least partly due to genuine sympathy for another man's problems. But he had to be honest.

"Maybe it wasn't an accident," he said. "Maybe this fellow couldn't bring himself to fight Indians and this was his way out."

"You're crazy," O'Hara said heatedly. "No sane man would do that."

"All right," Allison said. "Maybe he wasn't sane. Or maybe he didn't intend to die. He just figured on shooting himself enough to get sent back to Fort Fetterman."

"Why, why, why?" O'Hara said. "It doesn't make sense. No soldier would do that."

"Do you know what will likely happen to you if you're taken prisoner?" Allison asked. "You'll lose your hair and your life, of course. But have you thought that before you die, you might lose your balls, too? And maybe have an arrow rammed up your rear to boot? Think about that a while and maybe you'll shoot yourself in the thigh."

O'Hara's face turned so pale that his freckles stood out, bright and sharp. He said: "No, I wouldn't. I'll fix it so I'm not taken prisoner."

He walked away. When Allison turned, he saw that Johnny Morgan had been listening. Johnny's face was bilious green.

"Forget it, Johnny," Allison told him. "That might happen to a cavalryman on patrol, but not to us lowly foot soldiers."

But his assurance didn't help. Johnny Morgan went without his supper that night.

CHAPTER TWENTY-ONE

Walt Staley returned from Fort Fetterman with dispatches and a sack of first-class mail. He ate, he slept, and then Crook sent him back.

Staley had already worked beyond his planned month, but he couldn't quit now. Not with a big Indian fight in the offing, and couriers in short supply. Crook planned to surprise the Sioux, but Staley saw that as a futile hope. Indian scouts must have reported all troop movements to Crazy Horse soon after they began. Staley didn't doubt, either, that small bands of Indians, probably Cheyennes, were still raiding between Forts Fetterman and Laramie. The danger of Tally Barrone's brothers turning her over to the Cheyennes was as great as it had ever been. Tally was never out of his mind, but he could not quit before Crook tangled with Crazy Horse.

He left after dark, wondering once again if he dared risk seeing Tally. This was a constant temptation, but the answer never changed. For one thing, he could not spare the time. Crook had ridden a short distance with him when he'd left camp, giving him advice that he didn't need and emphasizing the urgency of getting the dispatches on the wire. He wanted General Sheridan to know exactly where he was, and that he expected to find Crazy Horse's village west of the Rosebud.

The Crows had not arrived yet and he needed them to scout for him. He would move fast and hard, once they came. And, of course, he wanted the dispatches that would be waiting for him at Fetterman.

Staley rode through the dark hours, guided by the stars. Dawn was showing in the eastern sky when he caught the smell of wood smoke. Gold seekers would not stray this far off the Cheyenne–Black Hills road. Crook was not expecting reinforcements. He must be close to a band of Indians.

Reining up, he studied the ridge to the west. The breeze that had brought the smell to him came from the west, so the camp must be on the other side of the ridge. He put his horse up the slope. He had better find out how big a bunch he was up against, and find out now. Within another hour or so one of the Indians would pick up his trail and the whole bunch would be after him.

Just before he reached the crest, he dismounted and crawled to the top. Lying flat on his belly, he looked down into the valley. The camp was there, all right, a camp for not more than a dozen braves. Three of them were with their horses a short distance from the camp, and just as he slid back, one of the Indian ponies nickered. His buckskin answered and he knew it was time to go.

He swung into the saddle and put his gelding

down the slope. When it reached the valley, he looked back. The three braves had topped the ridge and were barreling down after him, whipping their mounts at every jump. He went straight up the opposite ridge. His horse was shod and it could climb faster than the Indian ponies.

The buckskin took him up the ridge and over the top. He stopped, yanked his Winchester from the boot, and returned to the crest. Lying flat, he took aim and fired at the lead horse. The early-morning light was still too thin for accurate shooting, but he scored a lucky hit. He heard the solid thwack of lead striking the animal and then saw him stagger and fall.

The Indians started to shoot, but they had trouble locating him. He knocked over the second horse, but the rider of the third swung into a pocket, out of Staley's sight. He ran back to his mount, knowing that if he stayed, he'd be fighting a dozen braves instead of three. His job was to carry dispatches to Fort Fetterman, not to fight Indians.

He mounted and rode on down the slope, crossed the valley, and looked back. He saw a single brave on top of the ridge. The Indian showed no indication that he was coming after Staley, but it wasn't safe to stop yet.

Staley rode down the valley until he reached a branch of Powder River. He rode through the brush along the bank, followed the water for a time, and then reined up at the edge of the stream. He pulled off his saddle, watered the buckskin, then staked him out in the deep grass on the bank.

He felt reasonably secure now, with a screen of brush between him and the sage-covered valley. He ate a cold breakfast and lay back in the grass. For a time he simply relaxed and listened to the wilderness world waking around him—the chatter of magpies building a nest, ducks swooping down to land and splash a few yards downstream, sage cocks busy with the process of mating. Then he fell asleep.

The sun was almost down when he woke. He ate again, watered the buckskin, and as soon as it was dark went on his way. When he reached Fetterman before dawn of the third night, he woke the telegrapher and turned in his dispatches. He slept all day, picked up the dispatches that had arrived for General Crook, took another sack of letters, and headed back.

He returned to the command without incident, finding the expedition camped on Goose Creek in a wide valley. He saw that a party of Shoshones had arrived as well as the Crows. After turning the dispatches and mail sack over to one of Crook's aides, he ate breakfast. Then he walked across the grass to where a crowd of cavalrymen, packers, and Indians were whooping it up as wildly as a bunch of excited kids at a circus.

When Staley reached a break in the line, he

stared at the craziest scene he had ever come upon in his life. Some of the infantrymen were trying to ride mules. Obviously few of the walk-a-heaps had ever been in a saddle before, and the mules had never been ridden.

The whole valley seemed to be full of braying, bucking, kicking mules, and with soldiers hitting the ground and getting up and climbing back into their saddles and getting bucked off again.

Some of the soldiers took bad falls and groaned as they got up. Once in a while a man took a hoof in the pit of the stomach or his side, or had his wind knocked out. Then he was laid up for a while.

Staley felt sorry for Johnny Morgan. Johnny couldn't stay in leather for more than three jumps of his mule. Pete Risdon wasn't much better; for once the big man had more than he could handle. But Dave Allison stayed in the saddle, trotting his mule back and forth, as docile and well-behaved as if he were a trained riding horse.

Staley walked over to O'Hara. "What's this all about, Pat? Bill Cody gonna hire gravel-crunchers for a Wild West show?"

O'Hara laughed. "Buffalo Bill could use them, all right. I've seen his show and this one tops it. Say, do you realize mules can kick forward as well as backward? I've been watching some of them do it. They're fast and sneaky. . . ."

"I asked a question," Staley said.

"Oh, the general decided to mount his infantry," O'Hara said. "I guess we'll be heading for action tomorrow." Suddenly he clutched Staley's arm. "Hey, that big fellow there . . . that's Rice Peters as sure as I'm a foot high."

Pete Risdon had been bucked off again. He lay motionless for a few seconds, his wind knocked out of him. Then he got to his feet. For just a moment his eyes locked with O'Hara's. He wheeled and started toward his mule. The mule aimed a couple of kicks at the sky on general principles, trotted off, and stopped thirty feet away. He stood looking at Risdon, daring him to come on for another trial by combat.

"No, that's Pete Risdon," Staley said. "He's the man who was with me and Dave and Johnny the day we . . ."

"I should have guessed," O'Hara said excitedly. "Every time I visited Allison this fellow walked off. But that's who he is. I've got to tell the general."

Staley caught his arm. "Why? What difference does it make whether he's Pete Risdon or Rice Peters?"

"It makes all the difference in the world," O'Hara said. "Rice Peters is wanted for murder in Chicago."

"Don't tell the general," Staley said. "He's going to need every man he's got. He can't put Risdon in irons now."

O'Hara shook his head and jerked free. He started running toward General Crook's tent. Staley sighed. Nobody could reason with Patrick O'Hara at a time like this. Pete Risdon wasn't the only man in the command who had a criminal record. Why couldn't that damned O'Hara let well enough alone?

Later in the morning Crook sent for Staley, but the general said nothing about O'Hara or Pete Risdon. He simply told Staley to go back to Fort Fetterman, starting at first dark. Crook didn't know exactly where Crazy Horse's village was, but it couldn't be far away. Tomorrow would probably bring action—certainly the next day would—and he wanted General Sheridan to be advised of his progress.

Staley was tired enough to drop off to sleep at once. General Crook's aide woke him at sundown. He took the dispatches. He ate a good meal, saddled the buckskin, and started south again.

CHAPTER TWENTY-TWO

The command moved out early in the morning of June 16th. The men gulped down a scanty breakfast of black coffee and hardtack, then began the march, taking a north by west course. The cavalry led, then the pack train, with one hundred and seventy-five infantrymen on mules in the rear. The Crows and Shoshones rode on the flanks without any apparent order except that they followed their chiefs.

Allison was one of the few infantrymen who rode comfortably in the saddle. He felt a little stiff, but he had not taken any hard falls; his father had used mules on his farm. But to most of the others, mules were braying, biting, kicking monsters straight out of hell.

Johnny Morgan clenched his teeth against the pain that racked his body with every movement his mule made. Even Pete Risdon could not hold back a groan now and then as his big body swayed in the saddle.

The wagons and ambulances were left behind, along with part of the infantry assigned to protect them. No tents were taken. The men carried four days' rations in the saddlebags, one blanket, and a hundred rounds of ammunition in belts or pouches. Allison sensed grim expectancy in the air, a certainty that in only a matter of hours they would see Crazy Horse's village ahead of them and make their fight.

Allison didn't know for sure how many Indian allies rode with the command, but he guessed about a hundred Shoshones and maybe twice that many Crows. They made a splendid barbaric pageant, with the sun shining sharply on their guns and lances, their war bonnets nodding and bobbing as they rode. Some carried tomahawks made of knives with wooden or horn handles, as murderous a weapon as Allison had ever seen.

Allison noticed that the Crows were lighter-skinned than most Indians. He wondered if the high mountain air in which they lived had anything to do with it. Many of them were tall, and they seemed unusually good-looking even by white men's standards.

The braves wore shirts made of buckskin or flannel, breechclouts, and blanket leggings. Their moccasins were of elk, deer, or buffalo hide, and most of them carried bright-colored blankets. Their headdresses varied a great deal, and Allison grinned when he saw what they could do with an old Army campaign hat. They usually cut out the top and bound the sides with furs and feathers and sometimes bits of scarlet cloth.

The previous night the Indians had stayed up until a late hour making so much racket that Allison had not been able to sleep. Some of the noise was hard to identify, but it seemed to be a variety of groans and howls and shrieks that, along with the incessant pounding of their drums, was enough to keep anyone awake.

Allison wondered if they would be as anxious to fight today as they had been willing to express themselves the night before. But the Crows and Shoshones had suffered much at the hands of the Sioux. Probably they would be anxious to exact a savage and bloody revenge.

The command reached and crossed a divide, and at dusk made camp on the Rosebud. Allison took care of his mule, then helped Morgan and Risdon with theirs.

"I sure know what you mean about being better off in the infantry," Morgan groaned. "Maybe we couldn't have come as far as we done today if we'd been on foot, but I sure would feel a hell of a lot better." He stared sadly at his mule. "Dave, I swear he hates me."

As if to prove the point, Morgan's mule laid back its ears and glared heartily.

"How do you feel about him?" Allison asked. "Do you hate him?"

"Yeah," Morgan said in a low voice. "Do you reckon he knows it?"

"Sure he does. You can't fool a mule, Morgan."

"Then I'll hate the son-of-a-bitch out loud," Morgan said happily, and began to swear.

Risdon was unusually silent at supper. He

complained once about the hardtack being moldy, and then he disappeared. Shortly afterward, O'Hara stopped by.

"Dave," he said, "where's this man you call Pete Risdon?"

"I don't know," Allison said, "and what do you mean, the man I call Pete Risdon?"

"His real name is Rice Peters," O'Hara said. "Changing names to conceal your identity is nothing new in the Army. You can tell him he doesn't need to take off every time I show up. I know who he is."

"Well, who is he?"

"I said his name was Rice Peters," O'Hara said. "I knew him when he was a bouncer in a Chicago saloon. I mean, I knew his name and what he looked like, although I didn't know him to talk to. He's wanted for murdering his wife."

Allison didn't doubt O'Hara's identification, or that the man was capable of murder. Still, the news shocked him. He would never be Risdon's friend in the way he was Morgan's friend, but he had gradually learned to like the man. Pete Risdon had been a good soldier since Company A left Fort Laramie, and he would do his share of fighting when the command finally caught up with Crazy Horse.

"Well, what are you going to do about it?" Allison asked.

"Not a damned thing," O'Hara said angrily. "I

told the general who he was and all Crook would say was that he'd look into it . . . after the campaign."

"He's got other things on his mind, Pat."

"Like surprising the Sioux," O'Hara said derisively. "I was talking to Frank Gruard a while ago. He knows more about the Sioux than anybody else in the command. He lived with them for six years or so. According to him we won't surprise the Sioux. A hunting party spotted us today and by now Crazy Horse knows where we are. Why Crook ever thought we could sneak up on them is more than I know. Sometimes I think his reputation as an Indian fighter is all on paper."

"Does Gruard think they'll take a whack at us tonight?" Morgan asked.

O'Hara shook his head. "Not before dawn anyhow. We'll have pickets out. They won't surprise us."

Allison studied the reporter's freckled face in the thinning twilight. It seemed to him that O'Hara actually enjoyed the prospect of a fight. He had wanted to be with Custer's command, not Crook's. He had wanted to see action, fast. O'Hara might be one of those rare men who didn't know the meaning of fear. Or perhaps he was a fatalist, believing that a man should do what he could to protect himself, but if death came, that was his destiny and he must accept it calmly.

After O'Hara returned to Captain Hanson's tent, Allison sat up for a time, thinking about Christine, and his father, and his future, if he had a future.

Before he went to bed, Morgan said: "You've got Ma's address, Dave. If I'm killed tomorrow, you'll write to her, won't you?"

"Sure I will," Allison said. "But the odds are all in your favor, Johnny."

"I wish I could believe that." Morgan swallowed, Adam's apple bobbing. "But you know damned well somebody's gonna get it tomorrow. It could be me."

There was nothing Allison could say to that. But the boy had stopped running back at the hog ranch. He had finally found a source of courage in himself, and tomorrow he would fight, scared or not.

Then Risdon surprised Allison. He came close and said in a low tone: "I've got to talk to you, Dave. Nobody in the company has any reason to like me, but I always figured you and me could put on a fight that would be talked about for the next twenty years. Maybe you could lick me. I dunno. I aimed to find out someday."

"I never fight unless I have reason to," Allison said, and waited.

"I know," Risdon said. "That was why I didn't push you. Well, it looks like it won't never come off. Anyhow, there's something I've got to know. That red-headed reporter that hangs around you all the time. O'Hara. Has he ever asked about me?"

"He told me tonight you were wanted in Chicago for the murder of your wife," Allison said. "I didn't know whether to believe him or not."

Risdon was silent for a moment. Then he said: "I came home late one night and found my wife in bed with a son-of-a-bitch who had claimed to be my friend. I guess I went crazy or something. I beat hell out of the man, and when I came out of it my wife was dead." He drew a long, shaky breath. "What would you have done, Dave?"

"I don't know," Allison said. "I don't suppose any man knows until he's up against a thing like that."

"I figured O'Hara recognized me," Risdon said morosely. "What's he going to do?"

"He went to Crook, but the general said he wasn't going to do anything about it until the campaign was over. I guess for one thing he doesn't want to lose a good soldier."

"I'll bet he doesn't," Risdon said bitterly, "but as soon as he don't need me to fight, he'll hand me over to some sheriff and they'll send me back to Chicago and hang me." He slammed his big fist against his knee. "I'm gonna kill that O'Hara. He . . ."

"Cut that out!" Allison said sharply. "You just might beat that charge they've got against you in

155

Chicago, but if you kill O'Hara, you'll hang for sure."

Risdon's sigh sounded like a groan. "I'm going to light out," he said. "Maybe I'll have a chance during the fight."

He walked away, a tortured man. Allison wanted to call him back, but he didn't.

CHAPTER TWENTY-THREE

At 3:00 on the morning of June 17th the camp on the Rosebud was awakened by General Crook's order. The men took care of horses and mules, and cooked breakfast. By 6:00 they were on the move downstream, a long line of blue that seemed to go on and on endlessly as it bent back and forth along the Rosebud, a crooked, twisting stream now swollen by melting snow.

Through those first hours a strange, expectant silence held the command in its grip, a silence that continued during the march, broken only by the rumble of the stream, the thud of thousands of hoofs against the soft ground, the rattle of carbines and sling belts, and now and then the snorting of a horse. The infantry on the mules led out, but soon some of the cavalry moved past them.

Allison saw General Crook ride by on his black horse, carelessly dressed as usual in his floppy hat, hunting jacket, and buckskin trousers.

Minutes later O'Hara rode by beside Captain Hanson. He carried his carbine across his saddle, his short-stemmed pipe jutted from his mouth, and his black derby, now much the worse for wear after almost three weeks of campaigning, was cocked at its usual jaunty angle on his head.

Allison couldn't keep from smiling. Before the day ended, Patrick O'Hara would have all the excitement he wanted.

The country through which he rode was as pretty as any Allison had seen. Nobody could blame the Sioux for fighting to hold it. Pines were scattered on the bluffs on both sides of the stream, and grass spread a lush carpet on the floor of the valley. He knew now why they called this stream the Rosebud. The sides of the hill were actually pink because of the blooming buds of roses.

They reached the junction with the North Fork, which came in from the west, and followed the combined streams toward the east. Presently Crook gave the order to halt. Yesterday's march had been a tough one, and both men and horses were tired.

It did not surprise Allison to find Risdon still on hand. It would have been almost impossible to steal out of the bivouac area last night. The pickets had been doubled and it probably would have taken an experienced plainsman like Walt Staley to slip past them. In any case, Risdon was still here, his ugly, scarred face sullen. He had not said a word to anyone all morning.

Johnny Morgan had not changed, either. His face was white and strained. His eyes kept sweeping the hills, and occasionally he moistened his dry lips with the tip of his tongue. He said nothing. He didn't even act as if he wanted to look at Allison.

The veterans seemed to be taking the day in stride. At least they were disciplined enough to pretend that was what they were doing. Corporal Jones might have been on some casual patrol out of Fort Laramie, and farther downstream Captain Burt of H Company gave the impression that he was singing a solo on the stage back at the fort.

A band of Crow scouts rode in on the run and conferred with Crook. They had left camp before daylight, well ahead of the column. Now, from the way they were talking to the general, they were excited about something.

"Probably seen a shadow out there somewhere," Corporal Jones grumbled, "so they think Crazy Horse and his whole pack are coming in on us."

"Maybe they are," Allison said.

"Naw." Jones shifted his quid of tobacco to the other side of his mouth. "Hell, them Crows just play at being fighters. The Sioux and the Cheyenne, now, they're real scrappers."

Someone who outranked Corporal Jones apparently decided that the Crows had seen more than a shadow. Company A was ordered to fan out as pickets along the foot of the bluffs to the north. There they waited, the sun rolling higher into a clear sky. The morning grew warm, the minutes dragged, and nothing happened.

Shots sounded from beyond the ridge northeast

of the command. A moment later a Shoshone scout rode into the valley in a headlong run, screaming: "Lakota! Lakota!" Other scouts behind him raced toward the soldiers, yelling: "Heap Sioux! Heap Sioux!"

Indians boiled down out of the hills. Behind them other hostiles appeared along the crest of the ridge to the north until it seemed to Allison that the earth had given birth to thousands of them. Some were armed with bows and arrows, some with rifles. A good many carried lances. The Sioux war bonnet of eagle feathers seemed to float five or six feet behind the head of each warrior.

Many of the braves wore half masks made from the heads of wild animals, ears and horns still in place. Allison felt a sharp prickle run down his spine. The Indians sweeping down upon Company A looked like devils.

The attacking party of Indians rode with the skill and precision of trained horse soldiers. They were singing a war song, more of a chant than a song, in perfect time. Every brave had painted black and red stripes from the top of his head to his waist.

The infantry line held. The men kneeled and fired and loaded and fired again, and then they were ordered back toward the stream. Dust and smoke boiled up in front of Company A. Allison could not see more than a few yards ahead, but he could hear the roar of gunfire, the snapping of bullets past his head, the whisper of arrows, and the constant, terrifying yell of the Indians.

Suddenly the Shoshones and Crows charged the incoming Sioux. Allison heard one of the hostile braves yell: "Go home! We kill white men!" But the whites' Indian allies swept on. For a time it was savage hand-to-hand fighting, lance against lance, and tomahawk against tomahawk.

More infantry moved in. The line plodded up the slope to the plateau above the valley. The Sioux retreated, but Allison knew the cheer that rose from the soldiers was premature. The Indians would be back. That was the Indian way of fighting, to thrust and retreat, thrust and retreat, until the enemy broke and ran. After that, the massacre.

The infantry was joined by dismounted troopers from the 2nd Cavalry. They dropped belly flat behind a small ridge. When, later in the morning, the Sioux came at them again, the troops held their fire until the hostiles rode within a hundred and fifty yards. Then flame belched from the muzzles of hundreds of carbines and Long Toms, as the infantry rifles were called. The heavy fire broke the Sioux flood into two streams, both retreating to the north.

Allison reloaded. He took a long breath and looked at Johnny Morgan. He said: "Well?"

Morgan's round, dirty, sweaty, boyish face broke into a grin. "We gave 'em hell, didn't we, Dave?"

"That we did, Johnny. That we did."

161

CHAPTER TWENTY-FOUR

O'Hara was sprawled on the grass beside his horse when Company A fanned out as pickets. He knew that the Crow scouts had told Crook they suspected the Sioux were close. Still, O'Hara noted with surprise that no one seemed concerned. Probably the officers thought Crazy Horse's village was still a considerable distance down the Rosebud.

Crook was playing cards with his aide, Lieutenant Bourke, and several other officers. In spite of himself, O'Hara felt uneasy as he stared at the sky. Some of the officers were smoking. Captain Burt was singing. O'Hara only half listened to Captain Hanson's stories. Now and then he caught a few words from Tom Moore, the chief packer, who was relating one of his adventures to some of his men.

O'Hara sat up and filled his pipe. He lighted it, wishing Walt Staley were here. Staley might do more than Frank Gruard and the other scouts had done, but this seemed stupid, to sit here and do nothing when the Sioux might be just over the rim of bluffs on either side of the stream. George Armstrong Custer would never let himself be caught in this situation. He'd be leading his men down the Rosebud and doing his damnedest to find Crazy Horse's village.

O'Hara got up and started toward Captain Hanson. His mistrust of Crook had grown until he could not restrain it. He might be ordered back to Cheyenne if he spoke his piece, but that was what he wanted anyhow. If he hurried, he might get back to Chicago in time to talk that stubborn old martinet, Samuel Simpson Cunningham, into letting him join Custer.

Of course, there probably wasn't time now. Custer would be on the move before this and, if the Sioux whipped Crook as they figured to do, Custer would have the hostiles rounded up and back on the reservation by the time O'Hara reached him. He couldn't just sit and wait. . . .

Then it happened. The Shoshone scout, Humpy, rode in yelling: "Lakota! Lakota!" Crow scouts not far behind him were screaming—"Heap Sioux!"—and one of them was wounded.

After that everything got mixed up. The end of the column was still coming in when the shooting started. Cavalrymen saddled up and tried to get organized, with officers yelling orders and men cursing the horses and dust rising in a cloud that at times hid the rim to the north so O'Hara couldn't see what was going on.

General Crook mounted his big black and rode to the top of a nearby hill. Captain Mills also rode to some high ground to get a view of the attacking

Sioux, and all the time it was plain enough to O'Hara that if Major Randall, the Chief of Scouts, hadn't led the Crows and Shoshones against the Sioux and held them for a while, this would have been one hell of a bloody day.

O'Hara stayed where he was, sitting his horse beside the Rosebud. When the dust lifted enough for him to see the bluffs to the north, he watched the Sioux. They seemed to be pouring down every hill and up out of every gully. There must be ten times as many of them as Crook expected.

Staley had said that it was always a mistake to underestimate the Sioux. That was what Fetterman had done ten years ago, and he had lost his command as well as his life. Now, Crook was doing the same thing. For the first time in his adult life, O'Hara admitted that he was afraid.

He saw Captain Henry take two companies to the south bank of the Rosebud to prevent an attack from that side. Then he watched Colonel Royall lead two companies of cavalry up a side stream that flowed into the Rosebud a short distance above where the command had entered the valley. If he hadn't, the hostiles might have outflanked the infantry and wiped them out. All this time Crook was up on that damned hill.

Someday, O'Hara thought, *I'm going to write a book about this crazy campaign. And I'll place the blame for its failure right where it belongs . . . on the shoulders of a military spinster named Crook.*

Later—O'Hara had little notion how much later because of the shooting and smoke and dust and constant charges and countercharges all along the bluffs to the north—Crook rode down off the hill and assumed command. O'Hara stuck with Crook to see what he would do.

For all the shooting, it didn't seem to O'Hara that many men were being killed. There was more gallop than fight to this battle, and the Sioux warriors were like a band of wraiths—they were there, and then they weren't there.

It occurred to O'Hara that at least three fights were going on at the same time: Royall on the west, Van Vliet across the Rosebud on the south, and Crook in the center. O'Hara didn't say anything to Crook, but the general's view was blotted out by ridges and huge boulders, and O'Hara wondered how he could plan a battle from his position.

Suddenly, or so it seemed to O'Hara, Crook decided the battle was going well. He wanted Crazy Horse's village. The village had been his objective from the beginning. So he ordered Captain Mills to march down the Rosebud, forcing the horses to as hard a pace as they could stand. Mills was to capture the village and hold it, and later Crook would come with the entire command.

O'Hara joined Mills, because this was the kind of movement Crook should have ordered in the first place. The scout, Gruard, led the cavalry down the stream that made a sharp bend to the north. A band of Sioux occupied the bluff overlooking the west side of the cañon, but they were driven off by Troop E. After that Mills moved on downstream at a good pace.

Suddenly O'Hara felt better. The battle was moving as it should. If the village really was down here, and if they could capture and hold it, the fight would likely be over. The lodges would be destroyed, ponies captured, the hostiles' supplies lost. They probably wouldn't be wiped out, but Crook would win a victory, and Gibbon and Terry somewhere to the north could move in and finish the job. In a matter of days, the hostiles would be caught in a pincer movement. Then they would be disarmed and herded back onto the reservation.

The column halted about three miles below the bend where the Rosebud made a sharp turn to the north. Mills gave the order to dismount. Pine trees and large boulders made a thick cover on both sides of the stream. There was a narrow opening to the west, but suddenly O'Hara could see death waiting for all of them if they moved on down the creek into the confines of the cañon.

Major Noyes with five troops of the 2nd Cavalry had caught up with Mills's three troops. O'Hara listened to the conversation between Captain Hanson and some of the other officers, and he gathered that nobody was anxious to enter the narrow defile that lay ahead. The men rested their horses and tightened their cinches, tense and uneasy at the prospect of riding into an ambush.

O'Hara noticed that Gruard had moved away from the group of officers. He cocked his head as if listening to something that no one else heard. Then he nodded to the west and said: "There's firing yonder somewhere."

A moment later a trooper back along the line said: "Somebody's coming."

O'Hara heard it then, and he saw that Mills had, too. They waited, and presently Major Nickerson and an orderly rode along the column, Nickerson's magnificent black beard gray with dust.

"The general orders that you defile by your left flank," Nickerson said. "You are to fall on the rear of the Indians. Royall is hard pressed. Vroom's troop is cut up and Henry is badly wounded."

This accounted for the firing Gruard had heard. O'Hara knew that Mills had no choice. He would have to follow Crook's orders, of course. Glancing again at the mouth of the cañon, O'Hara was filled with mixed emotions.

If they had gone on as planned, they could march squarely into a deathtrap. Once caught in a crossfire—and they would be if Sioux marksmen lay hidden along the sides of the cañon—the column might be wiped out. Still, there was a chance that the troopers could get through, a chance the village was just below the mouth of the cañon, a chance that an important victory could be won within the next few minutes.

Here again, O'Hara thought, Crook was illustrating his timidity by calling Mills's column back before it had a chance to do what it had set out to do. But neither Mills nor any of the other officers voiced this criticism.

Mills led the way up the cliff, weaving back and forth among the boulders and fallen timber to the top. The climb was steep, and by the time the men reached the top, they were all blowing. They moved on through a scattering of boulders and wind-twisted trees, then came into the open, a grass-covered plateau that seemed to run on ahead of them for miles.

They had been leading their horses, but now Mills gave the order: "Prepare to mount. Mount."

O'Hara swung into the saddle and rode beside Mills. They swept out across the plateau—and, suddenly, there were the hostiles, surprised by an attack from the rear.

The men cheered as they charged. They wanted to come to grips with the Indians. But the Sioux look-outs sounded the alarm and the main body had no stomach for a fight in which the whites already held an advantage. The Sioux picked up their dead and disappeared to the northwest.

O'Hara glanced at the sun. It was about 2:00, so the battle had lasted six hours at most. What would have happened if Mills had been allowed to go on down the Rosebud? But he hadn't, and Crazy Horse and Sitting Bull and the rest were out there somewhere to the north, the Sioux village still intact.

Crook will go after them, O'Hara thought. *He's got to, and maybe he will catch up with them again.*

CHAPTER TWENTY-FIVE

The packers under Tom Moore and a group of Montana miners held a ridge in the center of the battlefield some distance north of the Rosebud. The infantry held another ridge to the southeast. Later in the day part of the infantry was ordered farther northwest to cover Royall's retreat toward the Rosebud. The rest of the infantry, including Company A, remained on the ridge.

It was just plain boring, Dave Allison thought, lying out here on his belly among the rocks, with the sun boiling down on him and his canteen empty and his mouth as dry as dust. Now and then he or Johnny Morgan or Corporal Jones would fire a shot just to let the Sioux know they were still there.

The Indians showed no inclination to charge the infantry with its "long-shooting" rifles, so Company A was not involved in the heavy fighting that had forced Royall back and had cut Vroom's troop to pieces.

From his vantage point on the ridge top, Allison had watched the charging and countercharging; he had observed how most of the braves carried two or three cartridge belts around their almost naked bodies. He had been interested, too, in the way each used a rope to tie around his pony directly back of the forequarters, and by taking a twist around either leg, fastened himself on the back of his mount.

The braves usually carried their rifles in their right hands, and their coup sticks on their backs in what looked like a quiver. Allison had heard Walt Staley describe the use of the coup stick. It seemed that a warrior gained virtue simply by touching his adversary with it. Staley had said that it made no difference who killed the enemy. The trick was to touch him first with the coup stick and thereby claim him. By modern white standards the custom made no sense. Without it, the Indians could have killed more whites.

The hours dragged by. Most of the time Allison listened to Morgan talk about his home and his parents and the dull life on the farm. At about 2:00 in the afternoon Allison saw Mills gallop in from the west at the head of his column. Within minutes the Indians began pulling out.

"By God," Corporal Jones yelled, "they've had enough! I'll bet the fight's over for today."

Some of the soldiers began to cheer. Johnny Morgan jumped up and waved his campaign hat and yelled at the top of his voice. His action was impulsive, the exuberance of youth, a victory cry as the Indians started to ride off the battlefield.

But somewhere out there a diehard brave had a long-range Sharps rifle that he had likely stolen from some white man. Allison heard the boom of the Sharps, a sound quite distinct from that of the Army rifles. He heard the thwack of lead hitting flesh and bone.

Allison kneeled beside Johnny Morgan. Blood poured from a gaping hole in Morgan's chest. The boy felt it and lifted his hand and stared at the blood dripping from his fingers.

"Write to Ma, Dave," he whispered. "Tell her I fought all right. I did, didn't I, Dave?"

"You sure did," Allison said.

Johnny Morgan died under the hot sun on a ridge top a thousand miles from home.

Later in the afternoon mules were brought up from the Rosebud to move the dead and wounded. Travoises were rigged up for the seriously wounded that could neither ride nor walk. Allison trudged beside the mule that carried Morgan's body. He helped dig Morgan's grave, surrounded by the fragrant blossoms of wild plums and crab apples. Morgan's body was wrapped in a blanket. The burial service was read, three rifle volleys were fired, and Allison picked up a shovel and helped fill the grave. Then, taking advantage of the fading summer sunlight, he wrote to Morgan's parents.

The camp came to life at 3:00 the following morning. The men hovered over cook fires, eating their breakfasts of bacon and hardtack and coffee, and in the chill, pale light of dawn, began their retreat up the Rosebud.

The column moved slowly because of the wounded. Near noon O'Hara rode up beside Allison. The reporter's face was a picture of concentrated fury. He said: "Where's the man who calls himself Pete Risdon?"

"I don't know," Allison said, "and I don't much care."

"He disappeared," Jones said, "and no matter why he did it. He's a fool. The Sioux will lift his hair before he gets to Fort Fetterman."

O'Hara chewed his lip. Then he said: "You know where we're going?"

"No," Allison said. "The general neglected to notify me."

"Well, I'll tell you," O'Hara snapped. "We're going to the base camp on Goose Creek and there we're going to wait for reinforcements." He cursed until he ran out of breath, paused long enough to fill his lungs, and added: "Just tell me why we aren't chasing the Sioux. We lost ten men killed and twenty-one wounded, so we're turning tail and running like a bunch of rabbits."

"We're short on ammunition," Jones said.

"There's plenty back here at the base camp," O'Hara said angrily. "We could pick it up and head back after the Indians. But, no, we're going to wait for reinforcements."

Allison wished O'Hara would go away. If he had to gab, he could do it to someone else.

"I didn't give the order, O'Hara," he said wearily.

"Of course you didn't!" O'Hara snarled. "If you were commanding this column, we'd be on the Sioux's tail right now instead of dragging back to camp like a bunch of whipped pups. Crook has the biggest and best-equipped expedition that ever went after the Indians in the history of the United States Army. Now he's had a little brush with them, so he's running away to wait for reinforcements. I tell you . . ."

"You've told us enough," Jones said. "Now I'll tell you something. I've seen too damned many smart-aleck reporters who throw in with a command like this just to second-guess the commanding officer. I don't aim to listen to no more of it. Get out of here before I pull you off your horse and kick your butt into the Rosebud."

O'Hara bristled, and for a moment Allison thought he was going to challenge Jones to do it. But then he dug in his spurs and galloped toward the head of the column.

"He's partly right, Corporal," Allison said. "I'd like to find the red bastard that shot Johnny, and I won't find him if we're going to sit on Goose Creek and wait for reinforcements."

"Maybe he's right, maybe not," Jones said. "The point is, the commanding officer makes the decision. That decision has to go whether it's right or wrong. It's no good telling the men it's wrong.

If I was Crook, I'd put that red-headed pest on his horse and head him for Fort Fetterman and tell him to keep going."

"He'd lose his hair like Pete Risdon's going to," Allison said.

"I'd cry," Jones said. "God, would I cry."

CHAPTER TWENTY-SIX

Walt Staley reached the base camp on Goose Creek with dispatches from Fort Fetterman on the afternoon of June 19th. General Crook had led his command into camp only a few hours before Staley arrived. He went at once to Crook's tent, but an aide told him he'd have to wait. Crook was having a conference with some of his officers.

The aide told Staley what had happened on the Rosebud.

"We won the battle," he added. "The Indians chose the field and left us in possession when the fight was over."

To Staley such a statement was ridiculous. The only way you whipped Indians was to chase them and destroy their villages and capture their ponies until they finally surrender. Then and only then could you return them to their reservation. As things stood now, the main body of warriors was intact to turn on Gibbon or Terry, if they came within striking distance.

"Of course this was not the decisive victory we hoped to win," the aide added fretfully. "Why do you suppose they quit that way?"

"Maybe they got tired of fighting. Maybe they were hungry. But they weren't whipped. That's the only thing you can be sure of."

"Well, we did win the battle," the aide said to encourage himself. Staley shrugged. That would be the claim made in Crook's dispatches, but Staley doubted that there was an officer in camp including Crook himself who was satisfied with the way the fight had gone.

The conference broke up a moment later. Colonel Royall, Captain Hanson, and several other officers left the tent, their faces grim. The aide said: "You may go in now, Mister Staley."

Hanson turned when he heard the name. He said softly—"Wait."—and strode over to Staley. He said: "I assume you will be seeing your reporter friend, O'Hara."

"I expect to, Captain."

Hanson hesitated, glancing toward the tent flap, then said: "Don't quote me, Staley, but O'Hara talks too much and too loud. As far as this expedition is concerned he has made himself *persona non grata*. It might prevent an unpleasant scene if he were to return to Chicago."

Staley understood. No one could control O'Hara's opinions as stated on paper, but they were just too much for the naked ear.

"He might be open to suggestion," Staley said.

"Thank you," Hanson said, and walked away.

Staley lifted the flap and stepped into the tent. Crook was seated on a camp chair, a packing crate in front of him serving as a desk.

"Glad to see you back, Staley. Any trouble?"

177

Staley shook his head as he laid the packet of dispatches on the crate. "None this time, General. I heard about the battle. I suppose you'll be here for a while."

Crook nodded. "I'm asking for reinforcements and ammunition. It was the lack of ammunition that prevented us from pursuing the hostiles. We can't move until it arrives."

"I'm resigning my job," Staley said. "I've worked now longer than I intended to." He paused, and then, seeing disapproval on Crook's face, added: "I intend to get married and I'm concerned about my girl's safety. She lives on a horse ranch between Fort Fetterman and Fort Laramie."

Staley had heard Crook described as more Indian-like than the Indians, but he had never felt the general was that way. He did not sympathize with O'Hara's criticism, either. The men in Crook's command would probably live a good deal longer than those serving under Custer.

Crook's blue-gray eyes softened. "You have reason to be concerned, Staley. We'll miss you, but I can find another courier. Go get some rest and a meal. I'm anxious to get this message on the wire to General Sheridan so he will be informed about our victory on the Rosebud. When you return to Fetterman, you will probably be asked to carry the correspondents' dispatches, also."

"I have a request to make, General," Staley said.

"I have a notion that O'Hara will want to go back with me, and if I could have one more man, we might make it fairly easy. Three rifles can raise so much hell with a small war party that the Indians will think twice before they hit us."

Crook's expression did not change when O'Hara's name was mentioned. Apparently he wasn't quite following Staley's thinking. At least Staley didn't think so, judging from his quizzical expression, so he added quickly: "I was hoping you would give Dave Allison of Company A permission to accompany us. That way we would have the extra rifle. His hitch is almost up and I understand he wants to go home."

"Request granted," Crook said, "although it seems to me that both O'Hara and Allison would do well to wait a day or two. I'm sending the wagon train back to Fort Fetterman for supplies. It will have an adequate guard, so it would be safer for them to travel with the wagons."

"It sure would," Staley agreed, "but O'Hara's anxious to get back to his newspaper in Chicago, and Allison has a father who lives alone on his farm in Illinois. I think they would be obliged if they could travel as fast as possible."

Crook nodded. "I understand. I suppose your friend, Allison, will want a horse."

"He'll need one, all right."

"This is not according to regulations, but I'll arrange it for him," Crook said, smiling slightly.

"Report back to me about dusk. I'll have the dispatch ready."

"I'll be here," Staley said, and left the tent.

Ten minutes later he found Allison squatting beside a fire with Corporal Jones and Al Cady and several other soldiers from Company A. Staley hunkered beside Allison and slapped him on the back.

"Glad to see you ducked when you had to, Dave."

"Uhn-huh. Have some coffee, Walt."

Staley took a cup from Al Cady, wondering about the tight expression on Allison's face. Corporal Jones nodded at Allison. "Johnny Morgan caught a slug in the brisket," he said.

"And Pete Risdon deserted," Cady added. "He'll probably lose his hair somewhere between here and Fort Fetterman."

"Well, I guess nobody's gonna cry over him," Staley said.

"Not like they will over Johnny Morgan," Jones said.

Staley sipped his coffee. Finally he said: "Dave, I made a deal with the general for you and O'Hara to go back to Fort Fetterman with me. I'm quitting, so we'll go right on to Cheyenne. The general said he'd see you had a horse. We're leaving about dark."

At first Allison's expression didn't change, then what Staley had said seemed to get through to him. He nodded. "All right, Walt. I'd sign up for another hitch if I thought I could square it for Johnny. But they'd probably send me to Fort Fetterman with the wagon train and then put me out in another hay camp."

"We'll hit 'em a lick for Johnny," Jones said.

"Just one thing, Dave," Staley said. "We may get into one hell of a tight squeeze before we see Fort Laramie."

"Good," Allison said. "I'll shoot me some Sioux."

Staley set his tin cup down and rose. "At dark," he said, and walked off to look for O'Hara.

He found the reporter in Captain Hanson's tent, scribbling hard.

O'Hara looked up and said cheerfully: "Hello, Walt. I'll have this story ready by the time you start back for Fetterman."

"You'll be carrying it yourself," Staley said. "You're going with me and Dave Allison . . . unless you're scared. I'll admit it's damned dangerous, just three of us out there in the middle of Wyoming with Sioux and Cheyenne hunting parties all around us." He paused. "Hunting for scalps, that is."

O'Hara jumped up, his face turning red. "I'm not scared! You know better than that. But I'm not ready to leave here, damn it. This is the worst-run outfit I ever saw. I mean to expose . . ."

"Patrick," Staley cut in, "I've already made

arrangements for you to go with me and Allison."

O'Hara's face turned from red to purple. "They can't shut my mouth about what happened on the Rosebud. . . ."

"Nobody is trying to shut your mouth," Staley said. "It's just that some folks are tired of listening to you. We're leaving at dark. You be ready."

"Is that an order from the general?"

"Just a suggestion, Patrick. All you have to do is go back to Chicago, expose the hell out of Crook, and then join Custer. Now there's a man who would never pull back because he ran low on ammunition. You'll just love it riding with old Yellow Hair. See you, Pat."

Staley walked off to get some supper and sleep.

CHAPTER TWENTY-SEVEN

Staley, Allison, and O'Hara reached Fort Fetterman early on a morning late in June, having ridden nights and hidden during the days just as Staley had done each time he carried dispatches. There had been no trouble, unless Staley's irritation with O'Hara could be called trouble, and that had not lasted long.

The first time O'Hara criticized Crook was the last time. It happened about ten minutes after they left the base camp on Goose Creek. Staley said O'Hara had better keep his mouth shut or Staley would pull him out of his saddle and whip him to within one heartbeat of his life.

O'Hara believed him. He sulked for a time, but he got over it by morning. When they reached the North Platte, he was in his usual good humor.

They crossed on the ferryboat, put their horses up the steep slope to the fort, and took the dispatches to the telegraph office. Staley thought that O'Hara would hold his until he had a chance to rewrite his account of the battle, having had time to cool off and look at it with a better perspective, but O'Hara said he couldn't afford to be scooped. He sent his story out on the wire with the others.

They slept most of the day, not waking until late afternoon. The men at the fort were anxious to hear about the battle. Allison did most of the talking. Staley had not been in the fight, and O'Hara, shooting a glance at Staley, announced that he'd been ordered to keep his mouth shut.

No one at the fort had seen or heard of any small band of Indians in the vicinity. This surprised Staley, who had expected some of the young braves, the Cheyennes at least, to splinter off from the main party and swing south, stealing horses and murdering miners, stage drivers, and passengers on their way to the Black Hills.

The three men bought supplies and rode out of the fort before dark, crossing the river again, and following the north bank. Staley tried to find comfort in the thought that the Indians must have moved north after the battle; if the Fetterman patrols had seen neither Indians nor Indian signs, there shouldn't be any Indians around here.

It was bad reasoning. Staley knew he was fooling himself, but he was not a man to do it for long. A dozen small bands could have passed without being seen. They wouldn't be looking for a fight with the soldiers, so they would make a wide swing around the fort.

As the night wore on, a sick worry grew in Staley. He should have taken Tally away from the Barrone Ranch. If she were dead—if her brothers had handed her over to Big Elk, she had probably killed herself by now—and Staley would blame himself the rest of his life.

After dawn, they stopped in a grove of cotton-woods and built a small fire of dry driftwood and cooked breakfast. Another hard night ride would take them to Fort Laramie. But Staley knew he could not hide here all day. They were ten miles, maybe more, from the Barrone Ranch. He had to see Tally, even if it meant fighting her father and brothers.

When he finished eating, Staley moved out of the trees into the open, his gaze sweeping the ridge top to the north. The problem was what to say to Allison and O'Hara. They should be safe if they hid until dark. By following the river, they could reach Fort Laramie sometime tomorrow morning. Tally was his problem, not theirs. He had no right to take them into a fight, and that was exactly what he'd have when he rode into the Barrone Ranch.

He started to turn back to tell them about it. Then he heard something flutter in the sagebrush downstream. He walked cautiously downstream, not sure what had attracted his attention. Probably some ravens had taken alarm and flown off, but he had to make sure.

He found the body of a soldier, his scalp torn off, his face dark and pecked at by the birds. He strode back to camp. O'Hara and Allison were lying on their backs, heads on their saddles.

"There's a dead man below us a piece," Staley said. "Hard to tell who he is, the shape he's in, but it might be Pete Risdon."

Both men jumped up. Staley said: "Better not go, Pat. He ain't pretty to look at."

"I'm not that soft," O'Hara said, and trotted after Allison.

He was softer than he thought. He took one look at the dead man's face, then staggered away and vomited. When Staley reached him, he ran his sleeve across his mouth, shuddering. He took off his derby and wiped his forehead.

"My God, Walt, that's an awful sight."

Staley nodded. "It is for a fact." He saw that Allison was on his knees beside the body, studying the arms. Staley scouted in a circle and returned to find Allison on his feet, O'Hara standing behind him, and staring in the opposite direction.

"If I read the sign right," Staley said, "there was about a dozen of 'em, maybe more. They didn't hang around here very long. They took his hair and his horse and rifle and headed east."

"It's Pete, all right," Allison said. "Not enough face left to be sure, but he's the right size and he's an infantryman. Besides, he's tattooed on both arms. A heart with an arrow through it on one and initials on the other."

"What were the initials?" O'Hara asked hoarsely.

"E.N.," Allison said.

"He murdered his wife," O'Hara said. "Or was accused of it. Her name was Edna Noyes before he married her."

"He killed her," Allison said.

"How'd you know?" O'Hara demanded, turning to stare at Allison.

"He told me," Allison said. "He came home and found her in bed with a man he thought was his friend and he went out of his head. He said he was going to kill you, but I told him not to. I said he might beat the murder charge, but it was the finish for him if he murdered you on top of what he'd done in Chicago."

O'Hara took off his derby again because he had begun to sweat again. "Finding him was one of the things I was supposed to do, but I didn't think it would work this way." He shot a quick glance at the dead man and turned his back again. "Hell, I should have let him alone. Crook didn't seem to care whether there was a murder charge against him or not. I don't see why he deserted. He must have known this would happen."

"He was afraid of hanging," Allison said. "I guess he was more afraid of that than he was of the Indians."

"We can't dig much of a grave for him," Staley said, "but we can't leave him out here. We can scoop out a sort of a grave in the sand."

Allison helped him carry the body to the sandy bank of the river. O'Hara stayed where he was. When they finished digging a shallow grave in the loose sand, they lowered the body into it and covered it, then piled brush on top.

Staley turned to look at O'Hara. The little Irishman had not moved. He was still staring at the distant ridge line, the hot morning sunlight pouring down on him.

"Come on, Pat," Staley said. "Catch up on your sleep and quit blaming yourself."

O'Hara walked toward the horses. He watched Staley pick up his saddle and lift it to the back of his buckskin. Then he woke up.

"Walt, what the hell are you doing?"

"I figured I'd let you two sleep today while I call on Tally. If I ain't back by night, you light out for Fort Laramie and I'll meet you . . ."

"By God, Walt," Allison broke in. "I didn't think you'd sneak out on us. We're into it together, all three of us. I know what you may find when you get to Barrone's. You're going to need our help . . . and I'll need your help when I take Christine out of that hog ranch. I don't want to go on to the fort unless I've got her with me."

Staley took a long breath. He should have known he couldn't get away with it. He said: "That band of Indians rode east. They're headed for Barrone's place. And unless we move fast they're gonna get there ahead of us."

They saddled their horses. They rode out of the trees and headed east.

CHAPTER TWENTY-EIGHT

Staley held a stiff pace, but he rode with caution.

Twice, when they crossed shallow streams, Staley told Allison and O'Hara to dismount and stretch their legs while he rode downstream, and then upstream, looking for signs. The first time he found nothing. The second time he saw tracks about fifty yards below where Allison and O'Hara stood with their horses.

Staley left his buckskin in the sagebrush above the wet ground that held the hoof prints of unshod ponies. He kneeled and studied them. Yes, there were at least a dozen braves in the band. The tracks had been made early that morning, perhaps four or five hours ago.

The Barrone Ranch was on the other side of the ridge that lay to the south, about half an hour's ride from here. Staley mounted and waved an arm at Allison and O'Hara to meet him on up the slope.

He reined up to wait for Allison and O'Hara. When they reached him, he said: "The Indians crossed where you saw me get off my horse." He jerked a hand to the south. "That's the direction they went. The Barrone Ranch is yonder just over the ridge."

O'Hara stared at him, not entirely following his

thinking, but Allison knew what he was getting at.

"You think they're at the ranch now, Walt?"

"I don't know," Staley said. "Big Elk is after Tally, but it's my guess his braves want horses and scalps a lot more'n they want to steal a girl for him. They may be tired and hungry, so there's a good chance they stopped long enough to fill their bellies. Nobody's chasing 'em as far as they know. It would be like 'em to stay there and sleep it off."

"Well then," O'Hara said, "let's ride down there and find out."

"We'll look first," Staley said, "and then decide. The trouble is, there's no cover going down the slope above the house. If they've got a guard out, they'll spot us."

"That's a chance we've got to take," Allison said.

Staley shook his head. "If they've got Tally, and we push 'em, they'll kill her. So we've got some figuring to do."

He swung his buckskin around and started up the slope toward the crest of the ridge. Just short of the top he reined up and motioned for Allison and O'Hara to do the same.

"Stay here," he said, "till I give you a sign."

He dismounted and handed Allison the reins. He ran toward the crest of the ridge, stooping, and then dropping belly flat and worming his way upward until he reached a place where he could look down on the buildings. He lay there a good five minutes, trying to make sense out of nothing.

There was simply no trace of life anywhere around the place. No smoke from the house, no one moving in the yard, not even a horse in the corral. This bothered him more than anything else. Louie Barrone always kept more horses in the corral than he needed. Even if he and the boys were out on the range, Louie would have extra horses in the corral.

Then, suddenly, he knew what had happened.

The Indians had come and gone. They had stolen the horses. They had killed Louie Barrone and taken Tally. Staley jumped to his feet and made a sweeping signal with his arm. He started running through the sagebrush toward the ranch, then realized there was no sense to this and stopped. He stood there, blowing hard, blood pounding in his temples, until Allison came with the buckskin. He took the reins and swung into the saddle. Digging in the steel, he rocketed down the slope.

He pulled up in front of the barn and swung down. The corral gate and the barn door were both open. He ran toward the barn.

He stopped in the runway ten feet from the door.

Louie Barrone lay on his back in the litter of the second stall, his head beaten into a jellied mass of flesh and bone and skin. A singletree lay in the straw a few feet from him, one end covered with dried blood and matted hair.

The old man had been beaten long after the last breath of life had left him, beaten until whoever had used the singletree had worn himself out. It must have been one of his sons, Staley thought, reverting to complete savagery as he took revenge for the brutal beatings his father had given him.

Allison and O'Hara stopped in the runway behind Staley. Staley whirled to face them. "Take a look in the rest of the barn. I'm going into the house."

He ran across the yard. The back door was open. He went on into the kitchen. The pantry shelves were empty. Flour and sugar sanded the floor. All kinds of litter lay scattered from one end of the kitchen to the other—pots and pans and silverware and broken dishes, stuff the Indians had knocked off the shelves and decided they couldn't use.

In the front room Staley saw that the guns were gone. The furniture had been turned over, much of it slashed by knives. He peered into the bedrooms. The same senseless acts of vandalism had been committed in each of them. And Tally was not in the house.

He stumbled outside. Maybe she was hiding in the willows below the house where he had camped the previous summer and fall.

"Tally!" he shouted. "Where are you, Tally?"

No answer. Of course there wouldn't be. They would have searched the willows. He stood with his back to the wall, head bowed, his last bit of hope gone. Then rage took him.

"I'll kill 'em!" he shouted, lifting his head and shaking his fist at the sky. "I'll kill Big Elk and every red bastard in his outfit! I'll chase them to hell and back! I'll . . ."

From what seemed to be a great distance, O'Hara said: "You're crazy. You're throwing your life away. Start using your head. There must be some place where she could go. Isn't there another ranch where she would be safe?"

Allison put his hand on Staley's shoulder.

"That's right, Walt. We don't know how much time she had. If she had a few hours' start, she might have got away. Maybe she made it to the fort."

"It's too far," Staley said. "There ain't nothing this side of Fort Laramie except the hog ranch."

"The hog ranch," Allison whispered. "My God, I never thought of it. And Christine's there." He shook Staley with all his strength. "Come on, Walt . . . let's ride!"

They ran to their horses.

CHAPTER TWENTY-NINE

Allison rode in the middle, with Staley far to his right and O'Hara far to his left. In this manner they covered a wide swath of prairie, the idea being that if Tally had escaped and was hiding in a buffalo wallow or a thicket of willows or a depression in the sage-covered ground, they would be more likely to see her than if they rode close together.

As he rode, Allison listened for the sound of gunfire. Fifi had often bragged that she had plenty of guns and ammunition, and any damned Indians that showed up would be sorry. But Fifi had more than her share of wind and he didn't really believe her.

Allison often forged ahead of the others, with Staley calling to him to slow down or he'd kill his horse. But it seemed to Allison that the miles stretched on and on and on, that they were no closer to the hog ranch than they had been at noon when they left Barrone's.

The sun had swung well over to the west when Allison saw the ugly, square house directly ahead. The horrible possibility that it had been burned and the women murdered had been in his mind all afternoon. But it was intact, with no Indians in sight.

Suddenly, magically a slim figure rose from the prairie in front of the three riders.

Staley yelled—"Tally!"—in a shout that could have been heard all the way to the hog ranch. He swung his horse toward Tally and dug in the steel. He hit the ground running, and swept her into his arms and hugged her and kissed her, their two bodies pressed so tightly together that they seemed to be one.

"I knew you'd come," Tally whispered. "I knew you would."

"Sure you did," Staley said senselessly. "Sure you did, girl."

Then an equally senseless embarrassment set in. He let her go and turned to the others.

"Tally, this is my friend Dave Allison. The red-headed one in the derby is Pat O'Hara."

She wiped her eyes, and sniffled a little and smiled.

"I'm pleased to meet you," she said shyly.

Allison touched the brim of his dusty campaign hat and said: "It's a pleasure, Miss Barrone." O'Hara took off his derby and made a sweeping gesture as he bowed.

Allison had never seen Tally before. He had not heard Staley describe her, so he had only a mental picture of a dumpy squaw. She was anything but that. Tall and slender and blue-eyed, she had a figure any white woman would envy. She was very young, of course—seventeen if Allison remembered right—but he saw a mature, beautiful woman in that dusty calico dress.

"Big Elk and his band are around here some-where," Tally said, turning back to Staley. "My brothers are probably with him. I suppose they went to the hay camp because they thought I'd go there. They'll be coming any time."

She moistened her dry, cracked lips with the tip of her tongue. "There's no use going to the hog ranch. I went there, but they wouldn't let me in. The big woman that runs the place said she didn't want any half-breeds in her house."

"The bitch!" Staley said.

"What is she?" O'Hara demanded. "Some kind of an animal?"

"Yes," Allison said. "That's exactly what she is. But she does have a house and we may need her to keep the girls in line."

"Maybe we can get to the fort," Tally said.

Staley shook his head as he stared in the direction of the hay camp. "We don't have time. There's some dust yonder. We'd better ride."

Staley stepped into the saddle. Tally swung up behind him, her skirt pulled high on her brown legs.

They watched the dust, taking it easy for a time because their horses were tired. But a few minutes later Staley said: "I guess they've spotted us. We better ride for it."

The Indians were coming in on the road that led

from the hay camp to Fort Laramie, and they were coming fast. Staley's big buckskin gradually pulled ahead of Allison and O'Hara. Even with his double burden, the buckskin was the best horse of the three.

The hog ranch was directly ahead of them now, and Staley yelled: "Open up!" Allison's horse was laboring. The animal would never make it. Allison pulled his rifle from the scabbard, and when the horse stumbled and fell, he jumped clear.

He yelled—"Go on! Go on!"—and kneeled in the sagebrush. He took a careful bead on the lead Indian and squeezed off a shot. The brave threw up his hands and spilled off his horse. The others angled off the road into the sagebrush.

Allison ran toward the hog ranch, his legs churning. He heard a bullet whine past his ear. Another tugged at the crown of his hat. Staley and Tally had reached the front door and were pounding frantically on it. O'Hara had taken the buckskin's reins and was heading toward the adobe corral. The Indians were coming in straight at the house, firing steadily—and still the front door of the hog ranch was closed.

When Allison reached the house, bullets were already slapping into the door and the wall. He yelled: "What's the matter with you, Fifi? Open up! Christine, make her open the door!"

He heard Christine's voice, shrill and deadly: "Open it or I'll shoot you where you stand!"

And another girl's voice: "If she misses, I'll get you, Fifi. We need those men inside."

O'Hara was coming from the adobe corral, running zigzag, his derby in his hand, his pipe in his mouth, and short legs pumping. The door swung open. Staley and Tally tumbled into the room, bullets snapping over their heads. Allison came next, diving to one side so he would have the protection of the wall, then O'Hara, scurrying on his hands and knees like a bug, shouting: "That crazy colored man out there won't budge! Says he's got to look after the horses!" The door slammed shut and one of the girls dropped the bar.

Staley and Allison whirled to the loopholes in the wall on each side of the door. Allison reloaded and fired, and Staley pulled the trigger of his repeater time after time. A shotgun boomed from the corral. Allison, loading again, saw Christine on the other side of Staley, firing a Winchester as fast as she could squeeze the trigger and lever shells into the chamber.

The Indians could not face fire as heavy as this. They broke and circled the house, yelling like devils and shooting under their horses' necks.

Two horses went down, their riders running for cover. Some of the other horses had been hit, Allison thought. Then the leader, a big buck mounted on a paint pony, pulled out of the circle and drew the Indians back out of range.

Staley leaned his rifle against the wall. He said:

"Tally, stay here." Fifi stood, spraddle-legged, in front of the bar, girls on both sides of her. One of them, a bosomy blonde, kept saying between sobs: "Let them come in. They're men. They won't hurt us if we treat them like men."

Staley strode toward Fifi. For a moment there was no sound except heavy breathing and the whisper of Staley's moccasins on the floor. Then Fifi said: "Who the hell are you?"

He didn't answer. He slapped her, and flesh made a cracking sound like the snapping of a dry stick.

"You bitch!" Staley said. "You wouldn't let her in."

He hit her again, and this time Fifi's head thumped on the bar.

"You didn't care whether the Indians murdered her or not," he said.

"I was afraid to let anyone in," Fifi whined. She flinched as Staley drew back his hand. "Who . . . who are you?"

"I'm Walt Staley and I'm giving the orders. Open the door, Dave. Shove her outside. Let her see how it feels out there in the open."

The bosomy blonde was still crying. "They're men," she sobbed. "Only men. Let them come in and we'll . . ."

"Shut up, Mabel," Christine said.

Fifi leaned feebly against the bar, hands palm down on the polished surface, face pea-green with terror.

"Open the door, Dave," Staley said, and dropped his right hand to the bone handle of his knife. "Open that door or I'll let her guts out right here on the floor."

Christine screamed: "No, Dave! You can't do a thing like that!" But Allison lifted the bar and yanked the door open.

"Walk, you bitch," Staley said. "Walk through that god-damned door or I'll run this knife up your behind and twist it."

Fifi drew a long, snuffling breath through her nose. She was biting her lower lip, biting until blood ran down her chin. And in that moment the bosomy blonde named Mabel bolted past her through the door. Mabel unbuttoned her blouse as she ran.

"You're men!" she screamed. "Men! I know what men want!"

She pulled her blouse off and threw it to one side and held her hands out toward the Indians. One of them raised his rifle and fired. Mabel spilled forward on her face and lay still.

The echoes of the shot died. The dust that had been scuffed up by Mabel's frantic feet slowly settled back to the dry earth. No one in the house said a word.

Christine closed and barred the door. She stood with her back against it, facing Staley. Allison went to her and put an arm around her. He said: "Walt, this is Christine. Fifi is her aunt."

Staley wiped his face, then swung around to face Fifi. "Get us something to eat." He walked to the loophole where he had left his rifle and studied the Indians. Fifi ran in her lumbering gait toward the kitchen. One by one, her girls followed her.

Christine put her face against Allison's shirt and began to cry. He forced her head back and kissed her, but she pressed her face against his chest again, nestling, crying softly. She didn't move for a long time.

CHAPTER THIRTY

For a time, Allison stood at the loophole beside the door watching the Indians. They seemed undecided about their next move. A band of ponies had been herded beside the road, but the Indians were just standing in a group, staring at the house.

The extra horses had probably belonged to Louie Barrone, Allison guessed, with perhaps some others stolen from the hay camp. The big brave who had led the attack stood a little apart from the other Indians, listening as they talked.

"What are they gabbing about, Walt?" Allison asked.

"Tally says that's Big Elk standing to one side," Staley said. "They're arguing about the next move, probably. They want the horses in the corral, but they ain't real anxious to pay the price of getting 'em. Big Elk wants Tally alive, and that makes a problem for everybody."

Christine remained beside Allison, her arm around him. "Let's get married," he said, "the minute we get to Cheyenne."

"Oh, Dave, it's all I've lived for since you marched off with Company A." She hesitated, then said: "You just got back in time. Fifi was planning on taking me to Cheyenne next week. I don't know what I would have done, Dave. I just don't know."

"You aren't worried about us?" he asked. "About our future?"

"Not one bit."

He laughed softly. "Neither am I."

"How long has it been since we ate?" O'Hara called across the room.

"We had breakfast," Allison said.

"That was a week ago . . . damn it."

"I'll go see what they're doing," Christine said.

She disappeared into the kitchen and came back in a minute. "We don't have any fresh meat," she said. "Nero hasn't been to the fort for a long time and he hasn't had much luck hunting, so we're having stew made out of bacon and potatoes and onions."

She pressed against Allison, putting her mouth close to his ear. "That friend of yours, the one in buckskin. He's a savage, isn't he?"

"I guess you could call him that," Allison admitted. "But he wants to marry the Barrone girl and he thought he'd lost her. It's a wonder he didn't, with Fifi turning her away from the door."

"I'm sorry about that," Christine said. She glanced at Staley, who was watching the Indians through a loophole. "He looks half Indian himself. Maybe that's why he scared Fifi so."

Allison grinned. "He sure had her buffaloed, all

right. If that crazy Mabel hadn't run out and got herself killed . . ."

"They're coming again!" Staley yelled. "Fifi, get your girls to the loopholes and start 'em shooting."

Fifi lumbered in from the kitchen. "Huh?" she said.

"Maybe they aim to burn us out," Staley said. "Or make a try for the horses. I dunno. But get your girls to shooting so they'll know how many guns we got."

"The girls can't hit nothing," Fifi said. "Nobody but Christine can."

"Get 'em to shooting, damn it!" Staley roared. "That's what counts. Let 'em hear lots of guns."

Fifi gathered her quivering bulk together.

"Sadie, get into the back bedroom. Laura, you stay in the kitchen. The rest of you come out here."

Allison watched the Indians. Big Elk was on his paint, giving orders. Suddenly they wheeled toward the house, Big Elk taking the lead as his braves followed him into the circle again.

Christine ran to the loophole she had used before. She slipped the barrel of her rifle through the hole and waited. The Indians began to yell, making obscene gestures, slapping themselves on the rump, waving their guns defiantly above their heads.

They made a savage and terrifying spectacle. All

were stark naked except for moccasins, breech-clouts, and headgear made of horns and bright feathers. Their painted faces made them even more terrifying, and Allison was not surprised when one of the girls on the other side of Christine went down in a dead faint, her rifle clattering to the floor.

"Pick it up, Tally," Staley ordered. "Everybody start shooting when they do."

Tally ran to the girl and pulled her away from the wall. She picked up the rifle and poked the barrel through the loophole. From the bedroom Sadie screeched: "Fifi, how do you shoot this damned thing?"

"Pull the hammer back!" Fifi shouted. She headed for the bedroom. "And then pull the trigger, you stupid . . ."

"My God," Staley said.

Outside, the Indians tightened the circle. Each brave dropped to the far side of his pony and began to shoot, holding to the pony's neck with one hand and riding with one leg over the horse.

Allison squeezed off a shot at one of the horses but failed to bring him down. He yanked the rifle out of the loophole, thinking soberly that there wasn't much of the Indian to shoot at. As he reloaded, a bullet came through the hole and slapped into the wall on the far side of the room. It would have killed him if he hadn't stepped to one side before loading.

Laura staggered through the kitchen door, holding her shoulder. "I pulled the trigger and the damned thing . . ."

"Hold it hard against your shoulder!" Fifi bawled. "Get the hell back into that kitchen!"

A moment later O'Hara, who had been firing his carbine as rapidly as he could, had his pipe shot out of his mouth. He swore and said it was the only pipe he had and how in hell was he going to get a smoke. Allison, reloading and firing, fought down an impulse to laugh. If he laughed, he might not stop. He had seen hysteria cases do that.

Now and then Allison heard the boom of Nero's shotgun from the adobe corral. He wouldn't be hitting anybody, but it was a good thing to let the Indians know someone was there. Once a brave took his pony out of line and rode straight at the corral gate. Again the shotgun boomed, and the brave wheeled and cut back into the circle.

Tally and Christine were firing steadily. The girl who had fainted had crawled across the room and was lying behind the bar. The others seemed to be spending most of their time trying to reload between shots.

Fifi went to the bar and picked up a bottle of whiskey. She raised it toward her mouth. A stray bullet shattered the bottle. She stared at the jagged glass in her hand and then, very carefully, she lowered herself to the floor and stayed there, motionless.

Big Elk shouted an order. A moment later all of the Indians were out of range. Staley put his rifle down. He saw Fifi and laughed.

"You'd better get her back to Cheyenne," he said to Christine. "She don't belong in Indian country."

"Neither do I," Christine said sharply. "Are they going to let us alone now?"

"I think so," Staley said. "They had to try us out one more time, maybe make us use up our ammunition. But being as we didn't run out, they ain't likely to hit us again. Burn us out, maybe, but not till it's dark."

"I'm about out of shells," Allison said.

"So am I," O'Hara said.

Christine leaned her rifle against the wall. "Fifi was too tight to buy much of a supply, so maybe the Indians will get us cheap the next time." She nodded at Tally. "Let's go see if the stew's done."

They disappeared into the kitchen, the other girls straggling after them. Fifi blinked and looked around. She put her hand down on a piece of broken glass and cut a finger and began to curse.

"Get up," Staley said. "Get into the kitchen. I'm sick of looking at you."

She staggered to her feet and blundered out of sight. Staley said: "Dave, how could a hog like that raise a girl as nice as Christine is?"

"It beats me," Allison said.

"It's simple enough," O'Hara said. "If a kid hates one way of life enough, he grows up just the opposite."

Allison frowned, puzzled. Then he grinned.

"You mean *she* does," he said happily.

CHAPTER THIRTY-ONE

The sun was almost down when Christine and Tally brought plates of stew and steaming coffee from the kitchen. Allison and O'Hara ate at the table, but Staley squatted near the door, getting up occasionally to glance through the loophole. After the last attack, the Indians had remained on the other side of the road out of rifle range.

An overcast had been working across the sky from Laramie Peak far to the west. The night should be black enough for the Indians to succeed in firing the house. They would hide in the sagebrush, and when the occupants fled from the burning building, they would be picked off in the light from the flames. Or, if the Indians failed to fire the house, the whites would use up their ammunition and die indoors.

Staley knew it was up to him or Dave Allison to leave the house after dark and do something—anything—that would stop the Indians.

After he thought about it for a time, he elected himself. Allison was a good man, but too heavy-footed to be out there in the darkness, trying to out-Indian the Indians. Allison would just get himself killed.

Tally had not left Staley's side since she had helped cook dinner, but they had done little talking. Staley figured she didn't want to live through the terror of her flight again, but she ought to know about her father. When he finished eating, and Christine had taken the plates and cups back into the kitchen, he said: "About Louie, Tally. We found him in the barn. He was dead."

Tally nodded wearily. "I knew it was going to happen. I told him, but he wouldn't listen. He never listened to me."

She paused, staring blankly across the room.

"Bill and Joe ran away from home soon after you left. They went with Big Elk's band and fought with the Sioux on the Rosebud. Then they came back and had a terrible quarrel with Pa. He threatened to kill them. He said if Big Elk or any of the Cheyennes showed up around our place, he'd kill both them and my brothers."

She brought her gaze back to Staley. "Bill took me off alone and told me Big Elk would be along in a few hours and he was going to take me. Bill said Pa couldn't stop it. I guess that was when I knew they were going to kill him. I didn't have a chance to get a horse, but I slipped out of the house as soon as it was dark. I had told Bill I was going to the hay camp where I'd be safe, and he laughed at me and told me what the soldiers would do. Maybe I should have gone to the fort, but I was afraid of the soldiers there, too."

He squeezed her hand. "You're safe now. If

anything happens to me, Allison will look after you. He's a good man, Tally."

"But he's not my man," Tally said. "You are. Nothing is going to happen to you. Pa's dead. Joe's dead, too. Allison shot him this afternoon. Before it's over, I suppose Bill will be dead."

Staley was surprised. He had seen Allison knock over the lead Indian, but he had not recognized him. Tally's sharp eyes had. It surprised him that she showed no grief. She must have hated her brothers, and her father had never listened to her and never really loved her. To Louie she was a housekeeper, no more and no less. She had not known love after the death of her mother, and that, Staley thought, was probably the reason she had turned to him so completely.

"Keep an eye on the Indians," he said. "I want to talk to Allison."

She rose and looked through the loophole next to the door. He walked to the table and sat down across from Allison. O'Hara grinned at him in his cocky way and said: "Well, I'm seeing some Indian fighting the other correspondents aren't. I'll scoop them after all."

"If you live long enough to get it on the wire," Staley said.

"Oh, quit that," O'Hara said. "We're safe inside the house. After a while the Indians will get tired and ride away. I was scared this afternoon, but not now."

"You'd better be," Staley said. "As long as Big Elk's in charge, the warriors will stay right where they are until the wagon train comes by. If the train's got enough of an escort to look tough, they'll pull out, but that may be a week. They'll have us burned out a long time before that . . . unless we get Big Elk. He's the one that holds 'em together. If he was dead, they'd probably break up and drift away."

O'Hara's eyes narrowed. "Is this the straight goods?"

"I don't figure it's any time to bull you." Staley turned to Allison. "I'm going out after the girl's body. The light's thin enough now so they can't get a good bead on me, but I want you to keep me covered just in case."

"Maybe I ought to go out with you, Walt."

"No, you stay at your loophole. Some of 'em might have sneaked up close enough to have a good chance of hitting me. And another thing. You said this morning that we were all in this together. If I get rubbed out, will you look out for Tally?"

"Of course I will, Walt."

"Good." Staley rose. "Now get over to that loophole. Close the door after me but don't bar it. I might have to get back in a hurry."

Staley lifted the bar and opened the door. The Indians were gathered around a fire on the other side of the road. They seemed in no hurry to go anywhere or do anything.

He left the house on the run, bending low, and almost reached the body before the Indians noticed him. He picked the girl up just as two of the braves fired. The bullets whipped past, missing him comfortably. Then he began running hard back to the house and the firing stopped.

Staley saw the door open ahead of him. He ran through it and heard it slam behind him.

"Where do you want me to put her?" he asked Christine. "In here," Christine said, and led the way into a bedroom.

Staley laid the body on the bed and Christine quickly spread a blanket over it. When Staley went back into the other room, Fifi was there.

"Where am I going to sleep?" she demanded. "That's my bed you put her on."

Staley put his gaze on the woman and his hand on the haft of his knife. Fifi went back to the kitchen.

"Tell her nobody's going to sleep tonight," Staley said to Christine. "I figure they'll try to fire the house before morning."

Christine nodded, and followed Fifi into the kitchen. Staley joined Tally beside the door.

"I don't look for that woman to live much longer," Tally said.

"I don't, either," Staley said grimly. "Not if I'm here very long."

He stared through the loophole. The light was so pale he could not make out the Indians. He thought about slipping out to the corral during the night and saddling the horses and trying to slip past them. No, he couldn't go alone, and if they all tried it, they would never make it. The only thing he could do was kill Big Elk.

CHAPTER THIRTY-TWO

The last lingering trace of color from the sunset had died in the western sky and now the night was totally black. Staley would have preferred to wait until after midnight, but he couldn't risk it. Big Elk's patience was frayed. The Cheyenne wouldn't wait that long to make his own move.

Shutters had been placed on all the windows and a lighted lamp on the bar gave out a murky light. Staley said to Christine: "Blow out the lamp when I tell you to." And to Allison: "When I get back I want in, but be damned sure it's me you're letting in."

Staley looked at Tally. He stood there, trying to fill himself with the sight of her, and then he kissed her and turned away. He nodded at Christine, who blew the lamp out. He opened the door and slipped through it and pulled it shut after him.

He left his rifle inside, because it would only be in his way. His knife was in its casing and his revolver was in its holster. If they weren't enough to do the job, it wouldn't be done.

For a moment he stood listening while his eyes became accustomed to the darkness. He heard nothing except the snorting of horses in the adobe corral and Nero speaking soothingly to them; he saw nothing in the blackness that surrounded him except the pinpoint of light on the other side of the road.

If the Indians were still gathered around the fire, he would have no chance to get at Big Elk. But he didn't think they would be. They were much more likely to have thrown a circle around the house to prevent anyone inside from slipping out and heading for Fort Laramie.

Staley guessed it would be this way for an hour or two until Big Elk decided it was time to fire the house. That had to be his plan. Nothing else promised the results the Indians wanted.

He started toward the fire, figuring it as the most likely point for Big Elk to be. He moved silently through the sagebrush, stopping often to listen. He dropped flat to the ground when he stopped, thankful for the covering blackness, then, hearing nothing, he moved on, keeping low, every sense alert.

Once he thought he was going to sneeze. He hugged the ground, his nose pressed against his buckskin sleeve. When the impulse faded, he went on, crossing the road and again dropping flat in the sagebrush.

The fire was dead ahead of him now. It was small, a typical Indian fire, but it gave enough light for Staley to see the only Indian beside it, a big man sitting with his head bowed as if he were lost in meditation.

Well, well, Staley thought, *Big Elk himself.*

Carefully he wormed his way toward the big Indian. All he needed was one more minute to reach him and drive his knife blade between the Cheyenne's shoulder blades, then slip back into the darkness. He didn't deserve luck like this.

Seconds later he dug his nose into the dirt, trying to make himself invisible to the Indian who had appeared out of the darkness behind him. Apparently the warrior didn't see Staley because he went past him, calling to Big Elk. The chief stood up and spoke arrogantly.

For a minute or so they faced each other, both gesturing and talking angrily. Then the brave seemed to be cowed by Big Elk. He stood still and listened. When Big Elk stopped talking, the warrior whirled and ran back the way he had come.

Staley had no idea what they had argued about. Maybe some braves were rebelling against Big Elk's plan, whatever it was. If so, Staley's time was running close, because Big Elk might find himself forced to make his move sooner than he wanted.

Staley inched forward until he was close enough to reach Big Elk in three long steps. Still he hugged the ground, waiting for the chief to turn back to the fire. He could not risk moving any closer, even though there was a tall sagebrush bush between them.

For an eternity the chief stood like a great bronze statue, the dim glow of the fire on his nearly naked body. Then slowly he made the turn, and Staley came up off the ground, the knife in his hand.

Staley took three long steps without a sound. His left arm came in under Big Elk's chin, jammed hard against his windpipe, and choked off his breath. Staley brought his knife sweeping in from the other side, and buried the steel hilt-deep, thrusting upward from the notch of the ribcage.

For several seconds the Cheyenne twisted and kicked and plunged in his desperate struggle to break free. Staley pulled the knife free and struck again, seeking the heart. Blood spurted from the wound and Big Elk went limp. Staley twisted the knife, jerked it free, and released his grip. The Indian fell beside the fire and lay still, blood turning his skin from bronze to scarlet.

Staley wheeled away, slipping his knife back into the casing just as Bill Barrone appeared in front of him, screaming: "God damn you, Staley!" Bill was dressed and painted like a Cheyenne. Staley would not have recognized him if he had not heard his voice.

As Staley drew his gun, the thought raced through Staley's mind that now his luck had really turned sour. He had to kill Tally's brother and the shot would bring the Indians down on him from all sides. But the choice was not his to make.

Young Barrone got in the first shot, the bullet ripping through the flesh under Staley's left arm. He brought his gun level and fired, the roar of his shot coming so close to the other that the sound was one great, prolonged explosion. His slug caught Barrone in the chest and slammed him back on his heels. He fell, his last word a curse that carried with it his terrible hatred for Staley and all whites.

Staley holstered his revolver and raced into the darkness. He would never tell Tally about this. It must have been Bill who had battered his father's head into a jellied mass of blood and bone. Bill, the elder son, who had been caught between two cultures and two opposite ways of life, who had favored one and hated the other, hated it with every nerve and fiber of his sick mind and his strong, young body.

Staley sprinted toward the house, feeling the sagebrush come alive with Indians. He heard them yell, heard the shots that several took at the sound of his running steps. He slowed up so they would not hear him, and a moment later the shadowy bulk of the house appeared directly in front of him.

"Dave," Staley called, "I'm coming in!"

The door was open when he reached the house. He lunged through it and closed it and leaned against it. He stayed there, panting, while Christine lighted the lamp on the bar. Tally saw the blood on Staley's buckskin shirt and cried out.

"We'll get it bandaged right away," Christine said. "Take off your shirt."

"So they got you," Fifi said.

Staley took off his shirt. For the first time since he had come here he didn't itch to kill Fifi. Big Elk had been worth killing. Fifi wasn't.

Christine came with a bottle of whiskey. She poured it on the bullet hole and Staley gritted his teeth against the stinging pain. One of the other girls brought strips of white cloth and Christine put a crude bandage on the wound. It would do until he reached Fort Laramie.

"They'll pull out before sunup," Staley said as he carefully pulled on his shirt. "At least that's my guess. We want breakfast before dawn so we can travel as soon as we know for sure the Indians are gone." He looked directly at Fifi. "Christine is going with us. Allison needs a horse. We'll take one of yours and figure it's an even swap, your life and the lives of your girls for a horse. Christine will ride the horse as far as the fort. Your man Nero can pick it up there. Christine and Tally can take the stage to Cheyenne. Now if you want to see your girl married . . ."

"Married, hell!" Fifi snarled. She glared at Christine. "Are you determined to marry this soldier?"

"Yes," Christine said.

Fifi groaned. "God damn it, I went to a lot of expense raising you. I got a right to make something on you now that you've growed up. But no, you have to marry a soldier who don't even own a pot to . . ."

"Breakfast before dawn," Staley said. "A horse for your life, Fifi. Is it a deal?"

Fifi looked at his eyes, and then at his knife hand. "It's a deal," she said, and lumbered across the room into the kitchen.

CHAPTER THIRTY-THREE

Pat O'Hara stood on the cinders beside the track in Cheyenne and watched the train as clouds of smoke rolled away into oblivion and the end of the rear coach became smaller and smaller in the distance. He was a happy man. Only a few hours ago he had stood before a preacher with Walt Staley and Tally Barrone on one side and Dave Allison and Christine Smith on the other, and had doubled as best man for both Staley and Allison.

They'd had a wedding breakfast, and then O'Hara had given Staley his brown gelding and refused pay for him. Allison had given Staley the horse he'd taken at the hog ranch, and Staley had traded him for a pack mule. After Staley had bought supplies, he loaded up the mule and headed west with Tally, and an hour or so later Allison and Christine had caught an eastbound train.

O'Hara had considered taking the same train but then decided it would be better if he didn't. He'd lay over a day and write the story of his ride south from Crook's base camp and the fight at the hog ranch. He'd give Crook hell for sitting on his hind end up there on Goose Creek without making the slightest effort to pursue the hostiles.

Crook had practically drummed him out of

camp. By God, George Crook would be sorry he'd done it. Before Patrick O'Hara got done with him, he'd be the sorriest general in the United States Army.

Maybe, if O'Hara had any luck, he'd get back to Chicago in time to talk that old tyrant, Samuel Simpson Cunningham, into sending him out with Custer. O'Hara luck never stayed bad very long. Maybe he could catch Custer in time to see some real campaigning.

He went into the depot, puffing on the new pipe he'd bought in Fort Laramie. He hadn't seen a newspaper. He hadn't even gone through his mail that the hotel had kept for him. Well, one thing was sure, he thought. No one could tell him anything about the Yellowstone Expedition. He had been there. . . .

He stopped, flat-footed, the pipe falling out of his mouth. His gaze fastened on the headlines of a newspaper that someone had left on a seat: CUSTER WIPED OUT ON THE LITTLE BIG HORN.

For a moment O'Hara couldn't even move. The big, black print of the headline swam before his eyes. He closed his eyes and rested.

Sometime later he bent down and picked up his pipe and slipped it into his pocket. Slowly he walked to a window, the newspaper in his hand. He began to read, and gradually he became aware that he was reading the truth. Custer had divided his command. Reno had almost been overwhelmed, but had forted up on a bluff above the river until Benteen joined him. The combined force had survived, but Custer, attacking the main village, had perished with every man in his command.

O'Hara put the newspaper down. He rubbed his face with his hands, remembering his ride with Mills down the Rosebud. If Crook had not recalled Mills, the chances were that the column would have been wiped out just as Custer's had been. If that had happened, Patrick O'Hara would be dead.

O'Hara sucked in a long, sighing breath. He took his handkerchief out of his pocket and wiped sweat from his face.

This was indeed the summer of warpath between the Indians and the Army. In the high tide of its military power, the Sioux nation had defeated Crook, then turned on Custer and wiped him out a few days later.

In the end the Army would win. As Walt Staley had often said, the Army could harass the Indians and destroy their villages and capture their ponies and starve every band into submission. The Army would return the Sioux to their reservations, but the Sioux would never be whipped on the battlefield. In spite of himself, O'Hara admired them.

He folded the newspaper and went outside. He guessed he'd better not write what he'd planned to about George Crook. He wished he could change what he'd put on the wire at Fort Fetterman. After all, it was pretty hard to fault a man who had saved your life.

A strange, electric prickle ran across his scalp. He took off his derby and touched his wiry red hair. Well, the O'Hara luck had held. He still had his hair, even though it rightly belonged in an Indian lodge.

Dave Allison put his head back against the red plush of the seat and turned it enough to look at Christine. "Scrootch down," she said.

He obeyed and she kissed him.

"We'll make out," she said. "We'll tell your father I was working in Cheyenne when you met me. I was . . . well, I was a waitress in a restaurant. That's honest enough work. You'll go back to reading law and I'll keep house for your father. I'll work, Dave. I'll work hard."

She smiled radiantly, and then she began to cry.

"What's wrong?" Dave Allison asked. "Why are you crying?"

"Because I'm so happy," she sobbed. "That's why."

Walt Staley and Tally rode west out of Cheyenne, on across the Laramie Plain, and deep into the Medicine Bows. They had ridden slowly, without plan, stopping when and where they pleased and enjoying every minute of it. They were free. They didn't owe anything to anybody.

Now Staley lay on his back beside the fire staring at the sky, thankful that the bullet wound Bill Barrone had given him had healed and didn't hurt any more. He put his hands on both sides of him into the deep grass and listened to the roar of the creek that tumbled past just a few feet away; he caught the blue flash of a jay as it darted from one tree to another above him. Half a dozen foot-long trout lay beside the fire. Back in the timber a young buck hung from a pine limb.

He said: "Tally."

"I know," she said. "Your stomach is crowding your backbone and your tapeworm is yelling for fodder. I'm hurrying just as fast as I can."

"It ain't that," he said. "I been thinking."

"Thinking?"

"Yeah. I decided we couldn't live like this all our lives. We ought to live in a house, Tally. A home."

She came over from the cook fire and kneeled in the grass beside him.

"You mean you want to settle down and go to work? We can't have a home and children unless you work."

He sat up. "Work?"

"Work." She kissed him and pushed him back

into the grass. "Now I'll go finish supper while you think about your future."

He grinned as she moved back to the fire, as graceful as a young doe. He guessed he really could do some work for a wife like her.

ABOUT THE AUTHOR

Wayne D. Overholser won three Spur Awards from the Western Writers of America and has a long list of fine Western titles to his credit. He was born in Pomeroy, Washington, and attended the University of Montana, University of Oregon, and the University of Southern California before becoming a public schoolteacher and principal in various Oregon communities. He began writing for Western pulp magazines in 1936 and within a couple of years was a regular contributor to Street & Smith's *Western Story Magazine* and Fiction House's *Lariat Story Magazine. Buckaroo's Code* (1947) was his first Western novel and remains one of his best. In the 1950s and 1960s, having retired from academic work to concentrate on writing, he would publish as many as four books a year under his own name or a pseudonym, most prominently as Joseph Wayne. *The Violent Land* (1954), *The Lone Deputy* (1957), *The Bitter Night* (1961), and *Riders of the Sundowns* (1997) are among the finest of the Overholser titles. *Bunch Grass* (1955) and *Land of Promises* (1962) are among the best Joseph Wayne titles, and *Law Man* (1953) is a most rewarding novel under the Lee Leighton pseudonym. Overholser's Western novels, whatever the byline, are based on a solid knowledge of the history and customs of the 19th-Century West, particularly when set in his two favorite Western states, Oregon and Colorado. Many of his novels are first-person narratives, a technique that tends to bring an added dimension of vividness to the frontier experiences of his narrators and frequently, as in *Cast a Long Shadow* (1957) filmed as *Cast a Long Shadow* (United Artists, 1959), the female characters one encounters are among the most memorable. He wrote his numerous novels with a consistent skill and an uncommon sensitivity to the depths of human character. Almost invariably, his stories weave a spell of their own with their scenes and images of social and economic forces often in conflict and the diverse ways of life and personalities that made the American Western frontier so unique a time and place in human history.

Center Point Large Print
600 Brooks Road / PO Box 1
Thorndike, ME 04986-0001 USA

(207) 568-3717

US & Canada:
1 800 929-9108
www.centerpointlargeprint.com